The Wedding

Karin Irshaid

The Wedding Feast

סעודת הנישואין

مائدة الافراح

KIENER

The Wedding Feast

After Sharing the Same Table and Meal,
One Can No Longer Be Enemies.

Arabic Saying

مائدة الافراح

من جلس واكل على طاولة معآ، فلن يكن عدوآ بعد .

مثل عربي وحكمة عربية

Only her back can be seen and a slight movement of her arms.

Lea, she says and reaches for the meat. Time is a moment. Does time exist?

Time has been reduced to a mathematical pattern, so that you can find your way with the help of numbers. It has been and will be. But it is not present, she says, and holds the meat firmly in her hand.

She inserts the knife below the tendons and removes them generously. With brief, quick movements she cuts the strips into small pieces and puts them in the cat's bowl. Now she washes the meat. The reddish water drips into the sink. She holds the meat with both hands and watches it drip. She puts it on a cloth, pats it dry lightly and slaps it onto a board.

Times in-between, Lea, are possible at times. Everything is always in-between. Time is only a moment from which history flows. I will tell you everything, Lea, which I have seen and experienced, and you should also hear the stories which they told me in reply to my questions.

The knife is sharp. She raises her shoulders every time she bores a hole into the meat with the tip of the knife. In rhythmical circles she scatters the salt over the leg of lamb and rubs it in.

She carefully removes the bluish outer layer of the garlic

bulb, holds the firm cloves in her hand and picks off the thin membranes. White nuts crunch when they are cut into small strips which she presses into the holes until they completely disappear in the meat. She mashes the remaining strips to a pulp. The aroma makes you feel hungry. She crushes fragrant pepper, pimento, cloves and the black berries from cardamom pods in the wooden mortar. Her arms rise and fall. She stirs in a little curry and cumin, adds dried mint from a bunch, a few rosemary tips and olive oil to the crushed garlic.

The colour must smell good, Lea. The smell must intoxicate you beforehand, then the meal will be a pleasure. They used to dish up meter after meter. The table is measured in meters there, you can walk around it, you will hardly see the white linen because it will be covered with bowls, pans, plates and trays full of delicacies.

She spreads the spices over the leg with both hands, until nothing more can be seen of the meat. She lets oil drip onto her hands. And its colour changes immediately, becomes intense and brilliant. She rubs the meat evenly with her oily hands. She washes her hands but the yellowish-brown of the curry remains. They look henna-coloured.

Henna-coloured like the hands of the bride who sits for days before the wedding on a bed of roses and is painted with henna. This is the time that belongs to the bride, and it is properly celebrated. The time afterwards no longer belongs to her alone.

But this time before the hand-over from the one to the other is free and high-spirited. That's when the women are on their own. No man would dare to disturb them. They know that. And this sets the tone for their celebration.

With her hands she draws a circle in the air and points to the leg of lamb.

You must imagine the animal as a whole, I will roast only a part of it. At the wedding feast you have to show everything. You have to put on display what there is to eat. You will seldom find anything chopped-up.

She spreads green olive oil in the casserole, she peels the skin of a lemon thinly, cuts the fruit into thin slices and lines the casserole with them. She puts the leg of lamb on top, shallots around it and again lemon on top of everything, and a twig of rosemary. Everything is sealed with a big lid and pushed energetically into the oven.

Hasty movements of her hands over her jeans. The colour of the curry gives her hands a strange sheen and they continue working as if they were under external control. They grab the onion and lemon peel and dump them in the pail for the compost. With the cloth they rub the working surface clean again. Wipe, squeeze, dry, brush over the jeans, the hands rubbed together coming to rest for a while on crossed arms but become restless again and want to continue working.

She looks at her hands.

The henna painter who decorates the hands and feet with henna is well known in the family. You find this old custom, which the Egyptians knew about, in every religion around the Mediterranean. The good henna painter is like a good omen. She has her own recipes for mixing the henna. She won't give them away. She prepares it days beforehand with many wishes and sayings. You can imagine how carefully this woman is chosen. You put yourself into her hands. The red colour becomes a symbol of your happiness and should last as long as possible. The henna painter draws the smile of the moon and flying suns on the bride's palms.

If she draws them well the drawing lasts from one moon to another, and all this time the bride is the centre of attention and uses her hands as a sign.

Look, she lifts up her right hand with her fingers out--stretched and displays them like an identity card.

Close season from the family for a new family.

A lot can happen in this time. The time beforehand, the time in-between, the time afterwards. The time beforehand determines the time afterwards. After the time in-between you will always be on the look-out.

A glance out of the window. Look at the garden. The summer has reached the point where it tips over, where it cannot be more opulent and the green is laughing at the other colours. There are no empty spaces. It has grown rampantly with no empty spots. The branches, the twigs invisible, the paths covered in green, only the shape of the wall can be made out, the stones overgrown. The birds are silent. They have left their nests which have long since been devoured by the green. The summer is triumphant. It will die of its vitality, surrender and wait for time to pass. This repeated demonstration of power, Lea. She unscrews the lid of the tahini jar.

The starters are just as important as the rich main course. The colourful little bites attract the eye, are seductive, and the anticipation of the first bite after all you have seen beforehand, is great.

The fingers are ready, they grab, break the flat bread and push it with the colourful bites into the mouth. With eyes closed you test your appetite.

You have already enjoyed everything only by looking at it before you walk along the table in excitement to the little pigeons, the chickens, the stuffed pheasants and turkeys, to the bulging lamb with the lemon, garnished with parsley, in its open mouth. Everything is sorted by size and arranged in groups, one after the other. The food sways in waves over the table, like the eaters around it who cannot stop tasting it.

She scoops with a spoon the thick tahini out of the jar and puts it in a bowl with tender and skinned chickpeas. Adds garlic crushed with salt, lemon juice and a little water. She blends everything with the mixer. Takes a little of it with one finger. Licks it. Tastes it. Again and again. Adds a little lemon juice. A little more tahini? Some water. She stirs and stirs. The mixer is unbearably loud. It makes a bang into the silence of the room, cuts up sentences and only when the mass is reduced to a thick puree does the noise diminish.

She switches the machine off.

The hummus is ready.

Taste it. It must always be on the table.

She puts it on a flat oval dish, she makes a hollow in the middle with a spoon, puts some chickpeas inside and curly parsley around it. A little paprika dust in waves on top of it. Red, green, yellow. Into the hollow in the middle and around the edge of the puree she pours a fine streak of oil.

Hummus is part of every meal, of every feast. Even if you eat it every day. In the morning, at noon with every dish, and also in the evening it should be on the table with bread and olive oil. And every time and for everyone it tastes different. You never get tired of it, you will always ask for it time and again.

It is one of the starters that initiates everything. The starters prepare the ground just as the henna painter does with the bride. They excite and attract with their aroma and colour. A smile served up on plates. Not too much, everything should be cheerful and light. That's how the thrill of anticipation of the main course begins. Of laughing and fun at the table. It is only with the sugary cake and the burning candles that eating becomes pure pleasure. The dessert is like exuberance. The sweetness of the night.

Carefully and very patiently she removes the wafer-thin skin from the roasted red, green and yellow peppers and it lies transparent, almost without colour close by. The fruit has lost none of its colour as a result of the heat. As if undressed, the red, green and yellow strips lie side by side and start to glisten when they are covered with seasoned oil, put on the glass plate and then are looked at with amazement that so much colour has grown and is edible. Like the redness of the grilled tomatoes the flesh of which, freed from the blackened skin, mixed with a little salt, sugar, cinnamon and pepper, sprinkled with freshly plucked mint and oregano, flows into a bowl and lies so red, green with the red, green and yellow pepper strips beside the yellow, red and green spotted hummus dish.

A riot for the eye.

She washes the aubergines. The knife crunches into the violet and slices the furry white. The green courgettes spray with every cut and release a little juice before they fall into the hot oil with the aubergines, and, fried golden-brown on both sides, are laid on a plate where they are sprinkled with salt and sweat for a little while.

They constantly drink mocca. The small cups are always ready. I need a break, Lea.

She fills the tall coffee pot with ground pungent mocca. The aroma diffuses, stimulates deep breathing, sitting down, leaning back and relaxing.

Sugar, a few cardamom pods, water, and the spoon rings in the pot, the mocca spins in a circle, wells up, and the first drops hiss on the hob. Then she lifts the pot, curbs the foam, lets it well up three times again before the mocca is ready.

While you do this you must speak nice words into the coffee. Forms of wishes, because the most important thing

13

with drinking mocca is not the two, three sips but the palpitations afterwards, when images of your fate dry from the coffee grains on the edge of the cup and someone knows how to read them.

She pours the coffee with a small peak of foam into the cups.

You hand the cup with the thickest foam to whoever is dearest to you, lower your eyes silently and look with the first sip into the eyes of the dearest one. The foamy dream is being sipped audibly because the more foam there is the more intense the dream.

Two, three sips and you turn the cup upside down.

She puts the cups on the kitchen table, sits down on the chair and stretches her legs out. She sits there leaning back, sips the foam first and drinks the mocca in small sips until only the thick grounds remain. She looks at them critically and turns the cup in her hand in a circular motion so that the inner rim is blackened with the grounds.

That's the way to do it.

She turns the cup upside down.

You now wait full of impatience. You talk about small things, words spoken in passing. You can only think of the coffee grounds. You turn the cup to catch a glimpse of whether the rim is dry. But the black grounds don't dry so quickly. You need to be patient. You put the cup down again and wait.

There is always a woman who can read these images. She is then asked to do it. She will be coy, but will definitely do it, and everybody will listen closely to these words, to this voice which comes out of the images, and believe her words to be true. Because these images come naturally to you. Everybody listens. Everybody knows. Because everything can be read.

The henna painter is familiar with these images. She will be plied with mocca so that she keeps discovering new signs for the times to come. She will tell you what only you know, Lea, and you will hear what you sense, what you know and what you want to know.

She removes the cup from the table.

This is how the henna painter will take your cup, look into it and be silent. Then she will look into your eyes and start to read as if from a picture book.

She shows it to her, holds the cup in her hand and looks into it with a smile.

I see a path, Lea, she will say, and looks at you meaningfully. The path is long and has many branches. A mountain blocks the path, blocks the view. A menacing ladder leads upwards. The ladder is for you. You must climb up it. Up there there is a ready laid table on a plain. Many people are sitting around it. All of them are eating from the same bowl, they are very animated and engaged with each other. You will probably feel your hunger. Someone leads you to the table.

The henna painter will take breaks. She keeps looking from the dark images in the cup at you and scans your face with glances.

A tree in blossom bears ripe fruit. A bull comes out of the

crowd and brings you seven apples from a tree, which you take away in a basket.

There is a black house on the plain on the mountain. It has no door. But a small tower with a single window. A woman is standing in it and is combing her hair. She is looking with her dark eyes, waves beyond the mountain and calls the bull to her. He vanishes like a shadow in the house.

When the henna painter falls silent, she turns the cup in her hand to look for more images. She points with her finger into the cup and tells you what she sees.

Opposite the black house there is a bright one. All the windows and doors are open. You look at it and know your are welcome. In the sky above a cloud is sailing towards you. A bird is flying out with a message and bringing you news which you have been awaiting for a long time. A ship is sailing with you over deep waters. A land lies hidden in mist. A woman is crying, she is walking away across a field.

A cock is laughing and is sitting on a big heart. You are riding on a swift horse. An abyss. A bridge. The laughing cock. The flying heart. A storm in the middle of an open book, which lets go of its letters and starts to write anew.

She puts the cup on the table.

That's how the henna painter reads from your cup, or something like this. She is observing you closely, your face, your gestures, and is taking her time. You are hanging on her every word, assembling the images, which only you understand, and the woman keeps talking and you know that she knows everything.

While getting up from her chair again, she raises her arms, claps her hands and pushes the chair back.

You forget to think and are simply just there. You hear the true fairy tales and know that it has always been like this.

The women around the bride stoke up the atmosphere. Music sounds from the cassette player, their hips sway, their fingers snap rhythmically, their feet turn with the beat, stamp with the tip of their toes, their eyes flash and reveal the wishes which they all have.

There is singing and laughter and one of them will start to tell them how it was for her sister. For her neighbour. How it was with the cousin. He knew nothing and he could do nothing and the woman finally took over. And with the other man who could not stop and always ended up screaming.

The women leave nothing out. Each of them openly tells one story after the other. And her own story. They laugh. They cry. They imitate the men's voices, their gestures, first of all in a subdued voice, with their hand over their mouth, then becoming louder and louder encouraged by the growing laughter, they act out scenes from their lives. The children are there. They dance, play, they are exuberant or listen intently to the storytellers with glowing faces. They know the stories. They hear them again and again. Again and again as if for the first time.

The bride remains calm on this day. She is spoiled lovingly by the women. In the morning in the steaming bathhouse packed in hot, humid towels. Sweating, bathing, showering, massaging. Tufts of hair in all niches, in all places are removed thoroughly, the skin is smoothed with ointments. The crimson of the henna later lights up the entrance to the night. Finally hands move tenderly over her skin and spread perfumed oil until her body glows and you could see your image reflected in it.

The room for the henna painter and the bride is prepared. Delicious little titbits, orange blossoms. Rose petals. The cassette player for the music. Coffee. Cigarettes. Sweets. Everything is prepared. Everyone is moving around.

Only the bride remains calm on this day. On the following day she celebrates just as exuberantly and dances till the wedding day comes. But for the time being she sits on the festooned bed and extends her hands to the henna painter, then her feet, which she paints skilfully and wraps according to ancient tradition with henna following her own formula, so that the thickly applied pigment tinges the skin evenly. A test of patience for the bride, all night long until the following morning.

The bride remains calm. She listens to the stories which she knows but which have a different ring to them before her own wedding. The women dance around the bride. They make the night go more quickly for her. Not long after this, the women drape scarves or cloths around their hips. They unbutton their blouses and knot them together under their breasts. On the cassette player Feyrous sings colourful images into the room. Wishes sway with the rhythm of the clapping hands and wave into the dance. The women laugh with the singing. Their red fingernails are stuck in their hair like pins and lift it and let it fall across the face backwards with a skilful sweep. Their heads tilted back and in this bent position the breasts bob upwards. Their shoulders twitch and their arms swirl in spirals up and down. Long hair reaches down to their calves. Everything is swinging. Nothing stays in its place. The upper body falls forward, rises again and stretches higher than before and the fingers snap sparks into the room. There is something inviting about the hips and the arms. Bracelets, necklaces jingle, crackling sparklers light up the faces. Some sing and cheer the others on. The music becomes faster and faster and carries even the children along with it. Even the old, who suddenly grow out of their chairs, wave chiffon cloths into the circling dance. Their eyes flash, they show it clearly. They have forgotten nothing. They can imagine everything. Everything.

She gets up, laughs and clears away the coffee cups from the table with a few dance steps.

From the oven comes a faint hiss. A spicy aroma diffuses when she takes the roasting pan out of the oven and pricks the meat until the pink foam comes out. She puts some more water in it.

19

This takes a while, she says and pushes the roasting pan back into the oven.

In a bowl she mixes rice, a little minced lamb with pepper, salt and torn mint leaves. Green, freshly blanched vine leaves lie like a fan ready to be used. She sits down at the table.

A woman on her own, in an oriental kitchen, is lost. Without help it would hardly be possible to make a normal meal for the day. But you need this help not only for the cooking.

You need the company. The conversation. This is the way to keep control, to stay up-to-date, create or dissolve order, you hold the reins in your hand. You hear stories, which are changed, shortened or lengthened at will, and you are involved when new ones are created.

Perhaps this is why what you do is so time-consuming and complex, because there is always something to be taken care of. That takes time. Like the cooking itself.

A carefully chosen meal will be served later like a finished story, and eaten together.

Who knows, perhaps it will sometimes be used to regale someone with something. Who knows?

She takes one of the vine leaves, smoothes it gently with her hand, puts a little of the rice-meat mixture in the middle, lays the small tips of the leaves on top and starts shaping a small roll from the bottom.

Rolled in this way the leaves are placed in a circle in the pot on top of slices of tomato and onion. Garlic cloves, whole cardamom pods are placed between them, they are topped-up with broth and boiled until the rice is soft and the meat is well-done.

Who knows what else was wound up when the leaves were being wound up, Lea. Life's decisions are not infrequently made at the kitchen table.

After years of separation two sisters are now sitting together again at one table after they found each other in a foreign country.

Years of anxiety, years of searching, years of loneliness and longing, years of pain from humiliations and powerlessness in the face of the arrogance of power. Resignation in the face of helplessness which ends in waiting, with the hope that time will change things.

What do you do when one day strangers knock on your door because they were driven from the country which they thought was their home, and are now looking for somewhere to stay?

How can you refuse to accept victims who are standing in front of your house with a document in their hands which states that they have rights granted by God.

People who need your house for their peace. You will become the victim yourself, because you are in their way, in your house, on your land, because they want to plant the seeds of their peace, secure it, so they say. They want to have their peace only for themselves, share it with no one and make it blossom by forcing their peace onto your country. And suddenly you are no longer allowed to whisper the name of your country. You are no longer allowed to drink from its springs. You will become a servant in your country, you will lose your rights, as you have to give way to strangers who believe, because of their religion, that they have ancient rights.

As a servant you become the enemy if you are unwilling to serve. If you are looking for ways to escape, if you oppose the new power you will be called a terrorist. It is easier to fight somebody you call a terrorist.

Your humanity is being taken from you. You are being turned into a monster so you can be more easily destroyed. A victim is always holding a bill which has to be paid. And now there are victims on both sides.

I have learned anew how to see, Lea. He who atones becomes vigilant. I saw injustice on both sides. As a child you were in this country with your family. You left later. You haven't been back there for years. But you remember.

Even as a child you learned the word "enemy". I came in your country to erase this word forever, with an olive branch in my arms.

They showed me your country and the people who used to live there, who you called your enemies. They showed me the enemies' land and I saw the people threatened by your land.

I saw life in both countries.

Our faith is old, ancient, the oldest, our faith is law, they say. Our faith comes from faith, say the others.

Faith makes us impervious to facts.

We are in the present and everyone has a right to justice. An enemy of mankind is someone who makes enemies. I encountered human beings even in enemy territory. The have the same fears, hopes, the same desires as in your country.

She takes a sharp knife and carves a roast chicken into rough pieces. Yellow drops fall onto the board. Then she puts rice into a pot, seasons it with pepper, salt, cardamom pods and whole garlic cloves. She puts the pieces of chicken and crisply fried cauliflower on top, covers everything with chicken broth. Everything simmers slowly in the large pot until the rice becomes soft. Makluba, as it is called: What is at the bottom will be on top. Turned upside down. Here onto this plate.

She turns round and makes a movement of her arm at the same time.

Then she spreads her fingers, gleaming with fat. Bits of chicken under her finger nails. With a nail brush she scrubs her fingertips, then clears away a few things and washes the plates and pots left around in order to make some space again. She opens the lid of a jar of cream, dips her finger tips into the cream, a subtle fragrance, then she spreads it over her hands and rubs in the cream very slowly until it has been absorbed.

The black sheep has become a golden cockerel, Lea.

Kassim was the black sheep from the beginning because he came from a flock of black sheep. Now he stands there, on his new land, driven by strangers out of his own land and he tells us what it was like to have his fields burnt down. What it was like to have his water taken away because others needed it for their purposes, and to demonstrate in their way their power, with the riches they have stolen.

What it was like when groups of observers, tourists, onlookers travelling in buses across these lands, in order to witness how the soil had become encrusted on the one side and the soil stayed fertile on the other, and moreover water suddenly flowed into the desert and as a result crops, which had never been seen before, were harvested over large areas.

Nobody asked where the water had come from.

The onlookers were pleased. The onlookers pointed at those who let their land become encrusted. They nodded when they saw the crust. They nodded when they saw the fertile soil. They nodded when they saw the harvest in the desert.

These people who had let the soil turn to a crust don't deserve the land. Not if they let everything turn to a crust. Those who are obviously more capable, they deserve the land.

To put everything in order, everything green had to be taken out of the one land and put in the other. And so you can see clearly where everything belongs. Everything that is green has to do with the familiar order. Everything else is dull, is desert and has something to do with those who are incorrigible and let the soil turn to a crust.

The onlookers nod. Keep on. Keep on. Show us everything.

The blossoming orange groves. The old olive trees.

The onlookers nod.

The water thieves smile.

How nicely they let everything grow.

The trees. Ancient trees. How many hundreds of years old will an olive tree become? The trees are silent. Nobody asks the question who planted them and for whom.

They simply stand there and show their mighty treetops.

The roots can't be seen.

What father has planted them for what son? Very new fathers have suddenly brought foreign sons into the land and deleted the time before. What doesn't fit mustn't exist.

The onlookers nod.

And no one has asked why the water has stopped flowing on the abandoned land and the houses stand empty or why there is a gaping hole in the earth, where a house had grown before.

Those who leave their land and house don't deserve it.

The onlookers nod.

And they don't ask why there is a gaping hole in the dry field. Why Kassim's house, the house of his fathers, was blown up and the garden and the land were sown with mines and sealed. Why new roads run like arrows over the ancient fields and head for the white houses of the settlers, enclosed by walls. Walls which serve as wedges, set boundries for white houses, watched over by towers.

There are many gaping wounds in the field.

The onlookers ask no questions. They don't know why Kassim spent months in prison. Because he was caught secretly fetching his water. Because he could no longer bear the sight of the dry land.

Because he was making leaflets in his garage which called for resistance. Plans to get hold of his water and his land again. Because his garage in the end flew through the air like an enormous bird, when they sent a rocket as a greeting into his garage, where they thought he was when he was fleeing from the water thieves, who in turn had made him a water thief. And this bird scattered thousands of leaflets, when it unfolded its wings and the roof flew off with outspread wings. They became literally wonderful flyers, they flew through the air and stained the sky blood-red for minutes, then fluttered down, in flames. A rain of fire. The leaflets were carried through the air for kilometres, scattered by the wind and reached, even weeks later, as if by a miracle, destinations never reached before.

Kassim had survived. The fire-flying garage did not injure him.

His seekers found him at the well, at the spring which his grand-father had dug up on his field. They caught him, when, with bleeding hands, he cut through the rolls of barbed wire beneath the sooty sky, in order to clear the passage for the water he needed.

For him it was the last open pathway on his land.

With the help of his family and an adequate sum he escaped life-threatening imprisonment and was removed from the country after having been cross-examined for months. Deported to the valley of night.

Zigzagging in search of peace. Until he found it in the land which his fathers had stepped on some centuries ago to unite their own culture with the culture that was there, so that a happy blend, still recognizable today, could come into being, which seemed familiar from the first day and won his trust. And he found in the land, some thousand kilometres to the West, on the other side of the Mediterranian, a landscape which resembled the fields he had left. He found a wide fertile valley, bordered by protecting mountains, beyond the beaches, where it starts to become quiet again.

The land was carelessly ploughed and forgotten. Between the fields he saw a few lonely houses, which, however, had been abandoned for other reasons than the usual ones in his native land. This desertion had nothing to do with expulsion. But with immigrants. You could almost call them occupiers, who occupied the land along the coast, the beaches, the hills by the sea.

From the villages behind the hills on the coast people came freely from their fields to take part in the cultivation or urbanisation as these occupiers called it. Like diggers in search of gold the invaders rushed through the narrow lanes of the old harbour towns, in order to take them apart and to find gaps which they could fill with their concrete buildings, to have a guaranteed view of the sun, the sand and the sea.

Kassim looked at everything. He took his time and travelled at leisure through the land. On the coast he always walked through the narrow lanes of the small towns. He saw people in a rush filling the streets. He saw them on the beach, in groups on the sand, turning towards the sun. He saw houses on the hillsides facing the sea.

But behind the hills, in the shadow of the sea, it became quiet. The land was left fallow. It smelt good in the sun and slept. It was only on the high planes, many kilometres behind the coast, between green and grey mountains, that he saw the land again in wide, tilled fields.

Kassim nodded when he had seen everything and went back to the fallow land, to the field which at first he had looked at for a long time.

The farmer's son was happy when Kassim bought the fallow land with the old house from him. His family hadn't lived there for a long time. The son had reckoned from the beginning on the foreigners. Over the years they had come in larger and larger numbers and locked themselves up in tower-like dwellings, skyward, as near as possible to the sun. On plots where there used to be fishermen's houses concrete towers were built which rose up like chimneys with windows and offered a wide view of the sea.

The son was clever. Look at all these people, he said. They all have money in their pockets. They all spend the money. You only have to make sure that they put it in your hand.

He said this and pocketed the money for the land with the house from Kassim, to begin with, went back to his office and was pleased that he was able to sell the land without a view of the sea that had become inconvenient.

He told his father, who from now on would sit in the coffee house every day.

In the past the father had worked the land. That was a long time ago. The father nodded, drank to it with his son. He held the glass with the brandy in his stiff, crooked fingers. He didn't speak. But he clinked glasses with his son who emptied his in a single gulp, patted him on the shoulder and left.

At that time Joseph felt that he had made a good deal. He just wondered that there were foreigners who don't want a view of the sea.

When he went back to his office it dawned on him that Kassim had not come as a tourist and that the deal with him would not end with the sale of the land. Joseph had become a dealer. He was inquisitive and clever. His office was situated in a supermarket and, because the many foreigners had many questions, he put up a large notice above his door: "Office for all questions. In all languages".

Through the foreigner's questions he got to know their needs. Different languages were not a problem for him.

He didn't know Kassim's language yet. He was curious about his questions and hoped to find new answers for new deals.

She goes over the herbs with a mezzaluna. The stalks crunch. She keeps moving the parsley, coriander, dill and the mint leaves into the centre of the board and chops them finely to a puree. A fresh smell of leaves diffuses. Green juice trickles from the board, runs over the table like a rivulet and stains the lower seam of her t-shirt with a green spot. She presses the liquid from the herbs, pushes it aside, chops the onions finely and puts everything with salt, pepper, cumin and a pinch of chilli, into a bowl with boiled, stirred red lentils and soft chickpea mash. There is a slurping noise when she mixes everything firmly with her hands and forms little balls. They are fried quickly and with a hissing noise in hot oil in a big pot.

She opens the door wide onto the garden. The warm air from outside mixes with the air in the room and blows away the aroma rising from the cooker. She cuts pieces of flat bread, makes a slot in the middle with her finger, puts in a lettuce leaf, takes one of the brown fried falafels out of the pot and adds it. A piece of tomato, a slice of cucumber, some tahini sauce.

That's how it's best, Lea, straight from the pot, hot and crispy with bread. That's a meal like our curry sausage from a stall. But falafels are without meat, consist only of vegetables and herbs, are affordable for poor and rich.

You can vary it every day. Instead of lentils you can use brown, red or white beans or only chickpeas. You can use hot seasoning or leave the mild taste of the herbs. You'll never get tired of it. On the contrary. You will enjoy eating it, the more often you have tasted it.

She filled several small pieces of bread with the falafel. Fetches two glasses, puts ice into them, tops them up with Campari, a little water and a few splashes of lemon.

It's the colour, she says. I drink the red.

She sits down on the kitchen chair, brushes her hair from her forehead, she relaxes her arms and lets them fall onto the kitchen table, then lifts the glass, clinks the other glass and drinks a sip.

I have often sat like this and listened to the stories. The homeland of these people is their memory. Where they have left their glances, that's where their history is.

Kassim had only one chair to begin with.

That's all that had remained in the house. In the morning he put the chair on the space in front of the house, sat down and looked over his new land. What he saw was not that much different, from the landscape of his fathers. He saw the gentle hills, arranged in terraces, with trees waiting to be pruned, the red soil in the fertile valleys with fields, the furrows of which were overgrown with wild plants, where the green in the hollows became more intense and the dark colour of the earth suggested the presence of a spring.

On the horizon he sensed the haze of the same sea which

also gave the fields of his native land their morning dew. He certainly already saw the strawberry fields which were soon to ripen there over large areas, smelt the spicy air between the long rows of tomatoes, pictured the vegetable fields, the asparagus beds, the harvest of which would dominate the market, because he was able to harvest some weeks earlier and to be quicker than many other traders. He saw the fallow fields, grasslands and groves, which bordered on his land and he thought of flocks of sheep, a cheese dairy, a poultry farm and crates for eggs, chicken grills, lorries, the various buildings for the various purposes, thought of warehouses and offices and of many people and the dense crowd, stretching for many kilometres along the coast and he thought of the "Office for all questions. In all languages."

He had many questions and answers at the same time. He got up and left.

The first answer he was looking for would be a wife.

He wanted a wife. He wanted children in his new house on his new land. He wanted a family to find a motive to make his new land his homeland. The chances of getting hold of the sort of wife he wanted quickly were not very good. In any case she should come from his family circle so that he could be certain that the tradition he was familiar with was kept. She should speak his language. Not just the words.

He saw no chance in the new land of finding a wife. He was still unknown and he did not want to put himself to a very great deal of trouble, nor did he want to set his hopes on luck.

Besides he had to be certain from the beginning that the woman would trust his plans and be prepared to start a new life with him, even beyond the borders. He had no more time to waste. He had learned not to wait for luck. He preferred to take it into his own hands.

It was customary, according to the tradition of his land, for a man to look first of all among the women in his family circle. The family is big. Its history is long. A family with numerous relatives and many branches. Steeped in old traditions which are still meaningful. The deep roots keep people together and give the family security and self-confidence. Even beyond the borders.

But Kassim was the black sheep from the beginning.

His ideas, his efforts to keep and maintain his land, to defend it were also shared by all the members of his family. But his ideas and especially his efforts, have harmed his family, because he let himself be caught, so that some members of the family, after he had to leave the land, were summoned for cross-examination and troubled by suspicions and the investigations that followed.

No father gives his daughter to a black sheep.

On top of this, to a distant, unfamiliar land, without the protection of the family which could intervene if something should happen to the woman. You marry security, which you can see, but for the time being Kassim could only offer photos. He needed a courageous wife, who was able to trust him and to see what was not yet visible, who could decide freely.

Kassim knew his options. He thought about the widows in the family. He knew two of them quite well.

They were young women who had hardly been married and became widows shortly after the wedding. Perhaps one of them, because of what she had experienced, would have wanted to leave her country, of her own free will, because her husband had died because of the complications and consequences of foreign rule. Both women had to experience that foreign rule leads to resistance and the resistance movement creates oppression. Oppression, terror, and counterterror.

Terror makes all humanity disappear. On both sides.

The two cousins were schoolchildren when they were put in the foreigners' prison. It took only their name on a list of signatures protesting against changes in the curriculum by the civilizers and the distribution of these leaflets to have them arrested after inconclusive cross-examination.

They did not really cross-examine them. They demoralised them.

It takes only a few weeks, sometimes only days. It happens quickly. Like animals in a pen, humans are jammed into cells.

Forced during this time to be together with so many other prisoners in one room, that they can only remain standing, can only sleep by taking turns. No chance of escape. You are not allowed out for any reason. You have got to do everything in the cell. Your arrest doesn't have to last for long. They get through many arrests in a short time. You have to keep quiet about everything that happens to you, what you have seen or heard. You've got to keep quiet inside and outside the walls. But you don't keep quiet because of fear, but because of shame, and because you cannot bear the disgrace of what was done to you there as a human being. And when you don't manage to keep quiet outside, you are brought in again until you've learned to keep quiet forever. Even screaming to the world outside is useless. What you say is not heard in this country. Everybody hears you and looks away.

Both of them were behind walls. And when the cousins were outside again they kept silent for a long time. But shame and humiliation are painful.

This bitter period left them with no peace of mind. It had left them with injuries which were inside, injuries which could not heal. Their cries were suffocated and stayed deep down until one day they exploded.

In this world of masters they were not even servants anymore. They were nothing. They just did not exist. Without dignity. Without rights. The livestock was there. The field, the sky were there. The enemies, the inhabitants of the neighbouring countries were there. These enemies had their rights, their idea. They had something to defend, on the one side as well as on the other they had something to fight for. Everyone was aware of each other, if only as an enemy.

But they were no longer enemies. They had taken their existence as enemies from them. They had nothing more to defend. They had taken every right to exist, to act and think autonomously. They turned them into living dead. They took away the name of their people, so that it would be forgotten. They exchanged it for the name of terrorists, and made sure that everyone, even outside the country, thinks of the terrorists' land when they hear a bang. They were not only a people without a country, they were also turned into a people without a name. Into ghosts. Present but absent in a ghost land.

And nobody wants to hear about it. Nobody wants to know about it. But one day times will change and they will say again: and nobody admits to having known about this? There will be somebody left who hasn't forgotten anything.

History changes like the times. Borders will shift, walls will be demolished.

What was considered possible by our neighbouring countries, has developed further and will also become a possible way of thinking for others. Even if it takes time.

We look closely. And suddenly it is human beings we see on both sides. A people of mothers and fathers, of children, of women and men. Young and old. There will be sisters and brothers facing us and looking us in the eye.

The peace movement will become imperative for conquerors and occupiers. They will no longer need enemies to justify their actions, to be able to civilize, to make use of their elaborate defence system. Peace will be a fact. Peace will put an end to the striving for power, laws and borders will be obligatory. Peace will destroy the weapons, will remove the uniform of the enemy, remove their protective shield like a shirt. Everyone will stand there naked, forced to become a human being and realize that human beings who have a right to be there with the right to justice live on both sides.

The two cousins exploded on a day in early autumn. They had been on the move all day to look for hidden weapons in remote caves. There were caves on the estates of their grandfather, which had been used over the centuries as chambers for supplies, storage places, sheds for animals or the like. There were caves which were known only by one member of the family or a few, which were difficult to access and were well hidden. Or they were well-known but access was never permitted because of mysterious traditions or superstitions. Even going near them was avoided.

During the '67 war many inhabitants fled to the caves and found shelter from bombs, napalm and rockets. If time permitted, they hid all their belongings there to prevent them from being plundered, something which no house was spared.

It was only later that the victors found out about the caves. When the searchers realized that there were valuable things to be found, they had the caves registered. State-organized troops and private scouts competed with each other. For weeks and months crowds of surveyors went over the newly captured land, recorded it on their white measuring sheets, but they were more focussed on looking for caves. Scouting fever took hold. There was talk of treasures from the Canaanites, Egyptians, Persians, Greeks, Romans, Turks.

They all passed through this land for a longer or shorter period and left behind something which could now be taken.

A law was quickly passed which stipulated that valuable items were not allowed to be removed from the place by anyone unpunished, unless they could be registered, recorded and used again. There was talk of hidden weapons which had been forbidden for the conquered by the victors after their invasion. This is why they were looking not only for knives, forks, sabres, swords of the Canaanites, Egyptians, Persians, Greeks, Romans, and Turks, but for anything that could be dangerous. And because the conquered loved big knives and spicy kebabs, those knives and meat skewers were collected as well. Nothing sharp, pointed was permitted.

The victors were successful. They found many such caves. They found family jewellery, hundreds of years old, and were astonished. They found masses of gold and silver items, coins, and antiquities. They were astonished. They discovered unsuspected pieces of culture. This was not appropriate, this had to be forbidden. They are not to have what they have, and when they have nothing any more they can only be nothing. Could never have been anything. They did it to suit themselves. They also found the usable items: weapons, ammunition, war equipment from all sorts of wars, from all sorts of countries. While the profitable items were received with a triumphant smile, the weapons were removed by force of arms. There were convictions, houses were blown up, deportations.

But the collectors had forgotten that it was not the weapons which made enemies of the people. Disarmament has not silenced the people. They would have had to tear out their hearts.

Surprised by the sudden onset of the war many people did not have the chance to hide their possessions so that they could not be found. But the grandfather of the two cousins who had been shot dead in the first hours of the six-day war, was said to have possessed weapons and ammunition and to have kept them hidden and they were never found. Neither in the caves known to the family nor in other secret places which were repeatedly visited.

He must have hidden everything well. He must have hidden it not only well, but also have found the time to take everything to a remote place. Again and again the family came together to solve the puzzle of where these weapons were.

Early in the morning, when the grandfather heard on the radio about the enemy's approach, he thought it was one of these propaganda news items intended to create fear, which could be heard daily from all quarters, and he was not frightened to go to his fields and see how his crop was growing. He was not frightened either when the noise of airplanes became louder. He just accepted it. There were daily manoeuvres, sometimes more, sometimes fewer.

He was an old man.

He had experienced the final years of Ottoman rule, which had lasted for many centuries. He had endured thirty years of English rule. He had witnessed much. He knew that it was possible to put up with a lot even if it was unbearable. He knew that things were transitory.

But none of the foreigners ever touched the land. The people had to pay tribute, there was exploitation, but their land, their house, their dignity had remained untouchable.

The grandfather knew it from the beginning. Whoever comes and builds houses and plants trees wants to stay. The old man knew that. He had still greeted the enemies as friends. He had had to learn. He was on his guard.

He was an old man.

He went over his land every morning. Every morning he smelt the earth, bent down and grabbed the fertile soil, felt the dew, crushed the humid lump in his hand. For years he had seen the sun grow out of the hills every morning, behind the row of olive trees which earlier generations had planted. As on every morning he walked along the length of the field.

Still he saw the wide valley with its red fertile soil.

Still he saw the houses of his brothers on the heights opposite. He still saw the farmers on the plain with their tractors driving over the fields and he saw the workers standing together in groups.

The shepherd was still busy driving the flocks on this early morning from the plain up the hills to the olive grove, so that they would find shade because the day promised to become hot.

Still he looked over to the houses which were densely

crowded in the valley around a monastery with a small crooked tower and the mosque, which did not look much different, and heard the noise of the children who lined up in the small school playground for early morning sports.

And still he saw the women moving back and forth between the ovens, to stoke up the ovens for the bread of the day. He saw the smoke rising, first black, sinking into the valley, wandering and becoming white, until it rested over the houses like a veil. He heard the bus wheeze before he saw its long snout with its open hood crawl over the hill. He looked through the open windows into the bus and saw the farm workers and the children from the neighbouring village, who were about to get off and run noisily to the monastery school. The bus was late that day.

It was an interim period of the day. The night was old. It had fallen into the sea. The morning was pushing over the hills. The morning was fresh. It was the time to begin with the daily chores, the time in which the day began, but its course yet open and to be determined by the actions of each individual.

It was also an interim period in nature. It was the time between ripeness and the first harvest. The fields were full. Early in the morning the grandfather was driven out by the ripe fragrance. One more week, perhaps only a few days, and the big harvest would begin before the fields could be tilled a second time.

Once again he let his eyes wander over the fields.

He was content, and it will be the last contented gaze,

which will have lingered on these fields because only a moment later everything changed.

He turned round because he heard behind his back a dull rumbling, a metallic scraping between the usual noise of aircraft, which he recognized and which made his scalp tighten down to his neck, because he knew right away what was coming towards him. His eyes were as sharp as arrows. The sun was shining over the yellow field and lit up the black tank which moved, swaying over a hill.

It was not yet bigger than the tip of his thumb. And yet the grandfather knew that this tiny tip of his thumb was a threat to his life, his family and everything which had meant something to him on this land with all its inhabitants.

He turned around and ran into the house. His wife and his two sisters were sitting drinking tea. They had expected him at this time, as on every day after his morning walk, as they called it. Only today he came back more quickly. Miriam was frying the sheep's cheese the way he liked it. The small rectangular pieces were golden yellow, and the smell of fried butter spread through the room. The radio was on loud. The croaking voice was announcing propaganda messages as usual. Nobody was listening to it. It was only a noise.

When he stood in the door, and the women saw his face, they knew immediately what was going on. It was only a movement of his arms and Miriam dropped the pan and the others broke away from the lavishly decked table, which later, as if by a miracle remained standing almost undamaged among all the rubble.

The grandfather ran down the stairs into the basement vault, pushed the women into the secret passageway, which led through a cool storage room in the rock to a cave, where they would remain hidden together with the others who had fled for a week, and fetched his shotgun, which he had used thirty years before in the revolt. Then he went into the room with the big barrels, rolled one of them out into the basement passage as far as the basement door which led outside, pushed it with all his strength through the door and let it drop gently into a hole.

Only a few days before he had had the hole dug because Miriam was not to throw rubbish out the kitchen window onto the chicken yard, where the chickens buried and spread it around, to his annoyance. The hole was directly below the kitchen window. It was big and deep enough to collect the rubbish for some time. It was a good hiding place. If necessary he would dig himself in there.

When the barrel lay among the rubbish he jumped in afterwards. He lifted it and found the ammunition, the pistols and the hand grenades undamaged and well packed away. He charged his shotgun. He knew what to do. He put one grenade in the right pocket and one in the left of his djellaba. He took two of them to make sure. He knew that he would defend his land and his family. He knew that anything could happen. He was prepared.

The noise in the distance became louder. Now also the farmers in the valley, the shepherds, the women, the children, the workers, the bus driver would sense the noise as a threat. The old man thought of them. He couldn't see them any more. Propped by his shotgun he had climbed out of the hole, and, hidden by the rosemary bushes, he reached once again the front of the house.

From the hill he saw the thumb-sized tank, which was now as big as a fist, coming towards him. It was followed by two more tanks. The fighters in the sky screamed as they cut through the air, dipped into the valley which he had been able to look at peacefully a moment before. They pursued the tractors and fired black bullets onto the paths which exploded into infested clouds. The fighters had already disappeared, their screaming swallowed up by the stillness, for the moment of a breath there was nothing, only then followed a thumping noise out of the blackness. Flashes as in a thunderstorm, it rained black flames onto the fields, burnt up the fruit and the people, and the tractors shrank and became dark lumps.

The old man saw from his hiding place the blackened air, he smelt the burning of the fields, he heard the rattling of the tanks coming towards him. He saw them getting bigger. A black wall of steel.

He felt the missile of the tank like a storm near him. He heard the whistling before it crashed and lodged not far from him in an olive tree, which was said to have been there for a thousand years. He heard it splitting.

It takes an olive tree twenty-two years to bear fruit for the first time. This one was many times twenty-two years old.

It had survived for generations. The old man saw how the

missile bored through the thick trunk, tearing it apart. A sea of fiery blossoms set it alight and seemed brighter than the light. Then the tree dropped its branches with a creak. A dancing, burning burden which still groaned on the soil and finally collapsed with a shudder. It took only a few minutes, and centuries were turned to ashes. A black glowing stump remained which stretched its burning arms towards the sky.

The old man nodded.

The tank was now as big as a tank. Its target was the house. The old man behind his rosemary bush saw it come closer. The two other tanks followed at a distance. They drove through the olive grove and rocked like boats on a sea of young trees.

Calmly he raised the big shotgun to his shoulder. Next to the burning tree stump he saw clearly the dark observation slit in the tank. He took a deep breath, breathed out slowly and calmly, he remained completely still, took aim and knew that the shot had landed right in the heart of the tank. It hadn't bounced off anything, in the noise it had disappeared unheard. The gun barrel stumbled briefly, the tank came nearer another few metres and then came, as big as a rock, to a halt between rosemary bushes not far from his bush on the path to the valley.

The old man stepped in front of the bush, looked around and saw his house standing in silence. He tried to walk upright. He knew how little time he had left. He was an old man.

He walked towards the tank. The black gun barrel pointed towards him. It became bigger, a huge hole, he could see into it. He heard the other tanks. He heard them nearby. He could not see them. He was in the shadow of the first one.

The tree dropped its last flames, glowing fruits fell down and spread out. A pathway of fire ran with the wind down into the valley.

The old man held the ball tightly in his hand. He screwed up his eyes a little, and, knowing the right moment, he took his hand out of his pocket, managed to remove the safety cap quickly and with the certainty of a falcon he threw the ball forcefully and skilfully towards its target.

Life. Life lived, and time. The land. The wife. The family. The children and the children's children.

The root of the tree was burning and mingled with the fiery lightening that shot out of the tank with a bang.

The house stood behind him. It was still standing. The old man in front of it like a torch which had not yet been set alight. He saw the second tank turn away. It drove past the house and thundered angrily down to the farmers, the shepherd, the children, the women and the workers. Over his burning fields into his burning valley.

The third tank came directly towards him. He saw its blackness, he saw its fiery tongue which took hold of him, set him on fire and tore him with it towards his silent house, into his rattling house, which trembled when he flew through it, over the set table with the swinging crystal chandelier and flew out through the other side of the house into the peace of the eternal night.

Crystal glow by day, clear and delicate sounds and the

cracking of the rocks down into the burning valley, a cloud of dust which hid the house for minutes. After this there was silence. A silent house with two man-sized gaping holes facing the hot sky.

The old man lay mangled in the hole which he had got them to dig a few days before. On the seventh day, when the women could leave their hiding place, they found what was left of him among the dust and the rubble in the hole below the window. He was covered with the soil of his land. It became a place where they often lingered and talked to each other.

Later the two cousins met at this spot below the window. From here they looked down into the wide valley, over the groves, the fields. They talked about the grandfather. His death was a turning point leading to a new era. Nothing was the same as it had been before.

The day was cool. The daybreak was blue. It came up from behind the hills and spread over the sky. It happened very quickly. It became even cooler now. It smelt damp.

They didn't go into the house. Nobody went into the house anymore.

After they had found the grandfather, nobody from the family went into the house. They said the foreigners had watched the valley from there for six days. When the men of the family finally entered the house, it was said to be al-

47

most empty. The only thing they still found there was the table, everything else had been taken away or destroyed. The women refused to enter the house. It stood there as a memorial. It stood there like a skeleton.

The two cousins collected dry rosemary bushes which grew wild and rampant around the house, found branches and twigs of an old olive tree and laid them down in preparation for the fire. They often sat, sheltered by the house with its commanding view of the land, and spent the nights like this, sitting at the fire.

This place acquired for many a secret attraction. The shepherds gathered there, because it provided shade at midday and warmth at night, and with the fields lying fallow it therefore became good pasture for the animals. The young men of the family sometimes met there to forge plans. Only the old ones of the family avoided the place. They didn't go there anymore.

The cousins lit the twigs, blew into the fire so that it burnt quickly and brightly, then, in order to make tea, they put a few logs into the blaze so that the kettle remained stable. They both sat next to the hollow at the fire, warmed themselves up and whispered. They had once again looked in vain for the grandfather's weapons.

Was it a legend or was it true that the grandfather had a barrel full of weapons and ammunition? From where else could he have had the grenade? And where, if he had it, could he have then hidden it so quickly? The soldiers found only the shotgun in the bushes. They had searched the house and its surroundings – except for the grave. They hadn't left out a single centimetre.

But the cousins had heard the grandmother talk again and again about the barrel. It left them no peace. It kept buzzing around in their heads. They kept getting carried away by new speculations. They looked at the house, at the gaping hole that was left behind by the rocket. A fissured wound through which they could catch sight of the starry sky and the radiant glow of the new settlements of the foreigners.

After the death of the grandfather the foreigners had built their first huts in the old olive grove. This is our holy land, said the foreigners. The land was holy for everyone. But the foreigners had to possess it for it to become holy for them.

The cousins saw the signals from the watchtowers of the foreign settlement, which formed circles of light over the land. They followed the circles with their eyes and saw the other new groups of houses like leaping stars on the surrounding hills, joined together by the bands of light. While during the day the extent of the sprawl vanished between the green of the trees and the bushes in the vast landscape, at night it became clearly visible through the lights. The cousins looked over the landscape and thought about the grandfather's hiding place, about the many stories which were told about it.

They whispered. They stoked the fire. The tea in the kettle smelt fragrant. They had picked wild peppermint leaves and put them in the black tea. They took out flatbread from their bags, olives, tomatoes and white cheese. They sprinkled sugar in the glasses before they poured the tea. Warmed their hands on the hot drink. Ate. Talked. Drank.

Since they planned to spend the night in this place they took their sleeping bags out of their cases. Then they stoked the fire again. It was supposed to keep them warm during the night as well. So they rammed thick logs into the loose embers, which they could easily place in the fiery hollow. The soil underneath broke, gave way and let the fiery hollow sink deeper. The fire was dense and bright now, and blazed into the night. It blazed down towards the shepherd from the near-by village. The shepherd had known the grandfather, he had seen the tanks coming from the hill on the other side and had hidden in a near-by cave, from which he could overlook everything, and had survived. He often sat together with the sons and grandsons of the old man and told them what he knew. He knew a lot. He had seen a lot.

The cousins expected him. They like to listen to the old man. He always knew stories which they hadn't heard.

They sat close to the fire. They sat on the spot below the window.

One of them got up to put more wood on the fire. He looked for dry wood, which was lying behind the house. The dampness of the fresh pieces of wood hissed in the flames and made them glow green and blue. Glowing sparks blew up from the middle, like glow worms, and fizzled out in the night.

It happened quickly.

Sparks shot sharply and steeply from the fire. Suddenly the colour red. The hollow buckled, the soil exploded and spat out a huge fiery bubble. A firework followed and whistled lethally into the silence of the night. The black soil groaned and piled up to form pointed columns. Cracks scarred the field and split it over several metres. The red danced up and down and flowed into a smoking sea. The fire raged on, ate up the bushes and ran down the dry field.

The observers turned up straight away. They had seen the fire in the night. They knew of the fire pit and had shone spotlights through the gaping hole in the house. They knew who stayed there. They observed everything.

When the sparks banged like shots from the fire, they made a move. They drove in a jeep and it did not take them long.

One of them lay dead, not far from the fiery hollow on the spot below the window. They found the other one beside him, his terrified face buried in the soil. When he ran out staggering into the night and could not raise his exhausted arms, they shot him on the run.

They had surprised two terrorists, they recovered a cache of weapons, they could stop someone fleeing.

At the spot below the window a deep hole was gaping again. The grandfather's hiding place had been found.

The shepherd on his way up the hill had seen the grave been formed a second time. Hunched forward he went back to the village.

❧

The charcoal has an even glow. She has gone to the terrace to scatter it in the grill. She rubs the skewers in oil and pricks the meat, the onions and the peppers in turn. She rolls mince, strongly spiced with lots of parsley, ground onion on a board to form a thin sausage and puts everything on the grill. She goes back into the house.

I have often heard this story, Lea. As well as all the others. They tell it again and again so that nothing is forgotten. There are evenings when there is no end to the storytelling. When out of every story new stories keep coming. The young ones ask the old ones how it was. The children eavesdrop, listen and ask how it will be. The men speak of actions. The women are the mothers of thoughts and pass their yearnings onto the children.

A land full of searching children, full of talking men, full of courageous women and full of waiting widows. There are many widows in this land. There are also many temporary widows, because their husbands spend years in prison or sometimes simply disappear. The women are patient in this land. They have learnt how to wait and have learnt to cope with circumstances. They are the soul of the land.

When both women became widows through the buried weapons of the grandfather and through the force of arms of the foreigners, they went back to teaching in order to support their families with the money they earned. They were young and maintained the hope that everything could change one day.

His hope and instinct led Kassim on the right track.

When he had finished drinking the mocca he did not wait any longer, he had heard what he wanted to hear. He got up and left.

So both women were ready to get married again. The uncle had confirmed that. One of the two would take the chance. Kassim was certain of this. Both women were in his thoughts when he started on his journey to the border of his land which he, as an outcast, was not allowed to step on. The uncle had declared himself to be his advocate.

Kassim expected the answer when he was with relatives in the neighbouring country.

The answer came with his uncle.

The answer made fun of him.

The uncle started talking.

The first one saw Kassim outside in front of the door standing like a beggar. Not only the border lay between them. She knew Kassim. Everyone knew him. He was well-known. When she went to school he looked after the sheep. A shepherd.

When she was a student he ploughed his land. A farmer.

When she got married, his house exploded. He had let himself be caught. An idiot.

When her husband died he was in a foreign land. An outcast.

And now he was standing on the border with nothing in

his hand, but an idea about how the future in the foreign land, on a piece of fallow field could be. A teller of fairy tales.

There were many of them in her land. She laughed. The conditional mood did not interest her. She loved clear images and saw what was to be seen. Nothing. She said no and the uncle left.

It cost Kassim a whole month before he could ask the second woman.

He had set his hopes on Daliah. This is why he had her asked first. He knew her as a little girl. Saw her hours on end with her siblings on the veranda bent over books. Later he often saw her in the country learning at her grandmother's while she was studying. She was always carrying folders under her arm. She always had a smile in her face when he saw her. He always caught her smile and smiled back.

He knew that she knew what she wanted and had wished that she had known this of him and believed in him.

But Daliah loved security which was visible. And after Kassim had left his land he had, in her view, left her environment.

She laughed. A shepherd, a farmer, a storyteller with a piece of land far away.

She also laughed about Mona, who said yes a month later. Mona had always admired Kassim.

When she had to go to school he made a detour around it and went his own way.

When they were all studying he took care of his land. He was not one of those who talked big, he went for it and defended the land with his hands while the others looked on and made speeches.

When he had to leave the country he also escaped the constant terror.

Mona's wish for peace was great. Also the wish to leave the country after her husband's death became greater and greater, because of the daily pressure she saw herself exposed to.

A big ribbon swayed on her head, that's what Kassim remembered when he thought of Mona. At the wedding of her older sister she skipped towards the guests and lead them to the bridal couple. The ribbon in her hair was as big as her head. Its tails reached down to her waist. They fluttered behind her when she moved, stuck out on the sides, billowed out. The king and the queen celebrated a festival, Mona was the princess at her sister's wedding. Her fairytale world was full of colours. The sister laughed, the groom was king. The mother watched the princess. Once upon a time, it will come about that I'll be the princess, the child shouted and immersed herself in the game.

This was long ago. Mona could hardly remember. The game was soon over. A short time. And she tried to rescue herself from the time afterwards to escape the hopelessness. Far away from the land of the mourners.

Mona said yes. The others laughed.

The wedding festivities were brief. A narrow table on the border between the old and the new homeland. Her mother, her uncle, a few relatives. A silent party. Then Kassim and Mona flew off.

Dreams came true at the end of the journey. There was silence over the valley, stillness before the next terrors, but peace.

Mona stepped out of the house and knew that tomorrow would be like today. Stillness meant peace and she began to smile, relieved when she had thoughts reaching out into the future.

Kassim put chairs on his new field in front of his new house, sat down on the chair which he had found in the house and talked, with Mona at his side, to the few guests, the farmer's son, Joseph, his father and some cousins and farm workers who had followed him to the new land.

Mona looked at the green hills, at the red soil in the valleys and sensed the same sea on the horizon which she knew from her homeland. On the table was the home-made bread, home-made white cheese, the olives of the land, vegetables from their own field. Kassim had slaughtered a lamb for the meal, the perfume of the herbs drifted over from the grill, there were fruits and sweets, they drank the water from the spring, which Kassim filled into carafes.

She was familiar with everything, the foreign country was not foreign, she was at home in peace. She smiled through the long day and later handed Kassim the mocca with the thickest foam.

Kassim talked about his family, about his old and new land, about his ideas, his work and about what they would soon see from this table. They all listened. They all nodded, and the old farmer and his son shook Kassim's hand.

Kassim envisioned everything. His ideas did not arise from his dreams. They came from memory. He did not grow tired of talking about it.

Roses should grow on the path from the road up to his house.

And roses soon lined the path. They grew luxuriantly in every colour and formed a fragrant path to his new terrace.

A well was supposed to be constructed. The water of the well murmured out of a sculptured palm tree as tall as a man, flowed over fan-like leaves into a bright basin.

Vines were supposed to be trained over the terrace, climb up the house and provide fruit and shade in the summer.

Soon fruit was hanging ready to be plucked through the canopy of leaves. The filtered greenish light fell on the big table below, at which they all would find a place to sit in the evening. But one old chair in the middle should never be exchanged. From it one's eyes should wander in every season over the countryside and from it everything should be visible to the eye.

The strawberry fields in spring, the long rows of tomatoes, the fields of vegetables, the slopes of fruit trees, the olive trees with the sheep and goats under them and in between the delicate almond trees. On the other side of the valley, where the hills rose to form mountains, in the shadow of extended buildings, the warehouses, the cheese dairy, the chicken farm.

Never should a tree or a bush in front of the terrace block out the horizon. Because on the horizon you should sense the mist of the sea, which bound Kassim's old homeland to the new one. And one could sense the mist of the sea, one could smell it in the evening hours in the wind – up from the coast and in the early morning; before the sun rose and the wind blew a fresh breeze over the land.

Then Kassim would sit on the chair and wait for the sun to become visible and illuminate everything brilliantly for a few minutes before he set off to the sea, down to the road with the "office for every question in every language" which he had greatly extended with Joseph, the farmer's son.

The black sheep had turned into a golden cock.

He knew it and laughed about it. He sat down each time on his chair and laughed about it. From joy. And pointed with his arm to his land which had grown by a hill or a valley. He was delighted to show that he had succeeded in realizing his wishes. Except for Mona, nobody had believed him.

She fills a flat glass bowl with water, puts in the remaining vine leaves like overlapping scales. Walking through the garden she cuts the blossoms of roses, marguerite stars, some lavender.

The bench, a place to linger. The afternoon is waning. The sun sends speckled light through the leafy roof. Opposite a ripe field undulates around a hill, changes its colours in the wind. Small clouds scatter spots of shade, flying images which for moments darken the colours.

Abundance for the eyes, she says and points beyond the garden. The lushness of the season makes you drunk. Like heavy wine. Everything smells fermented at this time.

A moment which drains the senses. A sudden force of nature, always seems to risk going beyond the limits and knows no fear of failure. This bewitching landscape which is capable of concealing its wounds.

The cat is coming out of the bush. Long-legged, it is stepping through the grass, brushes around the bench, before jumping onto her lap, turns to form a nest and rolls into it. Glances through the green-eye slit, then it puts a paw over its eyes and starts to purr.

As a child I tried to memorise a particular flower at a particular hour. The sight of a lily, its perfume, never to forget it again. I ran to my room and tried with my eyes closed to see the flower, to smell it. Made it my memory-blossom in the night, out of fear it could be gone the next day, out of fear it would not come back the following year, would disappear forever for some reason and be gone and vanish in oblivion after the winter and become a white spot.

She grabs the basket with the blossoms and gets up. The cat jumps out of its sleep and disappears into the bush, from which it had come.

In the kitchen the blossoms are put into the bowl beside the vine leaves. The red of the roses, the white of the marguerites, the blue of the lavender, the green leaves. A summer bowl, she says, and puts it on the table. The aroma of the dishes, the herbs, the flowers in the warmth of the afternoon.

Mona and her sister will have certainly sat together and have been busy like this, when they started planning the wedding.

Kassim's table became bigger. Soon it wasn't only his children he could see grow up but he also offered room to those relatives who had to leave the country like him. Mona's brother Antonius came. After his studies abroad he could not move around freely in his country. His country had locked the door on him. He was no longer wanted in the divided country. It was like this for him on both sides. He not only exposed himself to danger, but, because of his different way of thinking and behaviour, also his family.

He had learnt abroad to think freely. And from outside everything looked different. From outside he saw on both sides a people oppressed and tried to mediate.

Our peoples are joined together by the same disease, he said, the present is always the heritage of the past and he saw the cure in discussion. By being together he found attention, listeners, allies abroad. They informed, wrote, clarified. But what was possible beyond the borders became dangerous when he was back inside the borders. The walls had become higher and the rifts deeper in his absence. Antonius spoke a language which was no longer understood.

There is a language which everyone understands, he said. When you say peace and want peace every language is understood. He was not understood. He became inconvenient. He risked too much on both sides. The word peace caused fear, was a threat because everyone attached his own conditions to it; no one was willing to engage in shared talks and concessions.

It was not long before his friends regarded him as a foreigner and among the foreigners his utterances made him suspicious. There he had been targeted and made to feel that he wasn't welcome.

Foreign powers meanwhile controlled the way of life in his country, and inhabitants of the occupied country returning home, who had spent time abroad, were no longer welcome.

Every day he had to report to the new authorities, Lea. Everyday he had to request anew his residency. To be allowed to live in his own country.

This means they make him dance. A dancing bear. He turns in a circle. He wriggles, and everyone watches him come back every day. He comes today and is ordered to come back the following morning. And the following morning they have forgotten him, and he has to remind them of his existence. He has to tell them his name. His father's name. They insist. They want to hear everything again and again. The whole litany. Everyday he has to rummage through his memory. Has to turn it inside out and invent fairly-tales so that they trust him, so that their faces look content, so that they let him go, so that they get enough. But they don't. If they get something they want more. If he comes in the morning, they prefer the afternoon. The afternoon gets postponed until the evening. He has to wait. Day after day. For the stamp on a piece of paper which states that he was born where he was born. There were lumps in his stomach. The anger a big lump. Woe betide him if he doesn't perform his little dance to their satisfaction, that's what they are waiting for. Repeat. Repeat. Dance, bear, dance! They pull at his fur until he is standing there naked. But it is still not enough. They want to lay him bare. They see the storm in him and wait for the lightening. The thunder is their business. Quick as a flash. They have their own kind of lightening rod. Ingeniously devised and cleverly invented. Their techniques are perfect. With them everything is perfect. They stoke up the thunderstorm. They need the heavy clouds, the gloomy light, the daily threatening weather forecast. It justifies their thunderous actions. Look, the massive clouds weigh heavily on us, they must be driven away. Driven away! And they all nod once again. Nod.

It's the clouds which grab attention. Nobody asks about the thunderstorms coming from different directions. They all nod and bend in the wind. They are waiting for the thunderstorm. Lying in wait. It will come. They are prepared. It will certainly come. When the thunderstorm arrives, the lightning will come. And then they make use of their thunder machines which sound the all-clear. Run riot. They create new currents, new thunderstorms. No one escapes their machinery. It hangs over everyone, even when he has long left the area of the thunderstorm. They are still there. They interfere. Their clouds shed light, have huge eyes and record every trace of your paths, because you are coming out of the thunderstorm area.

The vastness between the continents, the span between morning and evening are not sufficient to escape the dark clouds. For Antonius they were everywhere.

Huge eyes were immediately there when he opened his mouth abroad. They looked at him when he talked about his country, wrote essays and handed them round. When he collected money with comrades for those driven into the camps who nobody wanted to see, because nobody wanted to look at them, because one had to make amends for other miseries and the misery of the suffering upset them and did not suit them. That's how they live. How they live is how they are. Otherwise they would be different. Misery must not be equated with misery. The misery of the sufferers is self-imposed, contemptible and not real misery. They are demanding in their self-imposed suffering. A burden for others. The effort is worthwhile when misery, with our help, becomes noble. Look, here it is worthwhile. That's how it has to be. And the misery of the sufferers quickly dwindles to nothing under the aspect of nobility. Set free from guilt.

It did not help Antonius that he had friends and allies among his new enemies abroad. In the country, beyond the frontiers other laws applied.

When Antonius returned to his homeland, he not only had become an experienced engineer, he had also become an experienced trouble-maker for those in control and for his fellow countrymen through his political publicity work, through the peace movement to which he belonged. And there were no gaps in the clouds above, the layer of clouds was dense and on the brink of a thunderstorm.

The lightning, however, came unexpectedly. It came on a hot afternoon from the sea-blue sky. Antonius was on his way to pick up a niece and a nephew from school. No one let the children, particularly the small ones, be on the street on their own. The dangers of the street were glaring. It had been like this for years, in the morning the roar of the aircraft tore apart the stillness of the land, the fighters in the morning roared over the hills, practiced low-level flying, performed pirouettes over the minarets, the church steeples and schools in which the teachers screamed their voices off.

The streets littered with broken glass. The windowpanes burst, and because they kept bursting, they hung up plastic sheets over the holes in the windows.

Look, look, that's how they live. Not even windowpanes. Not even windowpanes.

And in the afternoon, at the end of school, the patrol of tanks in the terrified streets.

The children picked up stones and threw them against their impotence.

They hurled their anger at the hopelessness of their fathers. Reversed the thunderstorm, slayed the lightning with their thunder and screamed with irksome voices. The children of the hopeless resisted. Did not want to be hopeless any longer. Condemned dispiritedness and beat fear to death.

Who would want to remain quiet? The mountain stack began to totter. The avalanches of stone started moving. The children brought movement into the landscape of death. After the paralysis of the elders they started to take action. To the anxious trembling of the mothers was added the proud trembling of the clattering of the soles of the shoes of their resisting children, and also the trembling, full of foreboding, when they heard the screams of the injured and the mourning over the dead.

The battering stones were the siren call of the children, which not even the youngest ones could resist. The mothers prayed for hope which arose from fear in a land of helpless fathers. They prayed to be rescued by and for the children. Gone was the time of impotence, of humiliation and shame.

The mothers trembled. Their trembling, a proud horse.

The siren calls of the children went from house to house. The smallest ones hardly grown out of their cradles heard them. Nourished by the worries of the elders they set themselves free from their mothers' laps. A different life, they shouted happily and sang and danced and fought against the dangers of the street and became a new danger for the street.

But in order to protect the smallest ones, father, brother, uncle were sent to take them home from kindergarten, school, in the hope that dangers could be avoided.

When Antonius picked up a niece, a nephew from school, there was silence all around. He held them by the hand. They went down the narrow street from the school. The buildings were higher here than elsewhere in the town. The sky curved warmly above, and the sun drew a light line over the dark walls of the houses and into the street. The smells of midday. Through the open windows the kitchenware clattered. Screeching music from the radios. The children kicked a tin by turns before them, which rattled down the street. The little girl balanced as a tight rope performer on the seams between the stone slabs.

They turned into the main street for a short while, which led to the market.

The shops were tired, some had their iron shutters down, lay asleep. They crossed the main street, left it behind and turned into the street going uphill, with the cemetery wall on both sides. Over the high walls the green of the tamarisks was visible. There was an aroma of basil. The street was narrow. It divided the cemetery into the old and the new part.

Antonius at first heard a soft noise. It was still behind the small wood near the town. But you could still hear it. It quickly became louder and right away he felt the rumbling of the earth approaching like a threat. That's how he perceived it, although he was actually used to it since the armoured vehicles cruised through the town several times a day. He looked around. They were just coming out of the small wood. There were three of them. They drove one after the other at high speed along the main street.

They had just reached the first cemetery wall when rocks flew over it. He heard the banging of the rocks against the armoured vehicles. He saw burning tyres roll. The black smoke drifted, an acrid cloud, up the street and darkened it. He saw youths jump over the wall and run, throwing rocks, in the direction of the vehicles. For a moment the noise of the vehicles lessened, screeched and then he saw two of them briefly reverse and turn into his street.

Antonius grabbed the children's hands more tightly and ran up the cemetery street. There was no chance of escape. The walls on both sides were high.

Soon some youths had caught up with him and ran past him shouting slogans. They were trained. They were fast. The noise of the tanks rushed through his head. The children holding his hand stumbled. They were unable to walk on their own. He took them both under his arms. The street, a tunnel. The sky, a smoking tower. His shoes made of stone, as if with every step forward the distance to the end of the street became longer. The children in his arms were rigid parcels. They had stopped screaming. The rest of the youths overtook him. A swarm flew past him and had already disappeared behind the cemetery wall when he finally reached the corner. He didn't see the youths anymore. Probably they had hidden behind the gravestones and bushes. He turned round the corner into a narrow path, saw the niche in the wall. The gate. The iron gate was still swinging, set in motion by those throwing rocks. There was a threatening noise close behind him. Antonius did not dare to look behind him.

He heard a missile explode like a large balloon bursting. A whistle went through the bushes of the cemetery. The stones shook below his feet. The crunching behind him was the corner of the wall bursting. The armoured vehicles had run down the corner of the wall, it was in their way when they were turning into the narrow path. The rest of the wall beside him, a quivering lizard's back. The hole in the wall, open jaws. Antonius saw it out of the corner of his eye.

The children. Antonius lifted them over the swinging gate. Strangers' hands grabbed them and took them from him. He saw them being carried away. To safety, he thought, looked back and saw the first vehicle behind him. For a few seconds it appeared to stop then the driver continued deafeningly in the same direction along the wall and came directly towards him.

The drivers were playing their game. Antonius remembered youthful laughter coming from the vehicle. The man who was standing beside the driver was moving to the rhythm of the vehicle, swayed his hips as if he were dancing. The vehicles pushed the stones of the wall before them.

Antonius grabbed the wing of the gate in order to slip through it at the last moment. "Allah" was written on the gate and "Only God is immortal". Ornate letters, woven into each other. They were big, richly ornamented and held the gate together.

God or Allah stretched out an arm towards him, grabbed his hand and held it tight, pulled and did not let go.

When the wall collapsed and the stones were pushed together, Antonius was not quick enough. His left hand got stuck between the wall and the gate. Stones piled up against the iron gate. The vehicle had become wedged into the wall and pressed with its impact the wing of the divine gate into the stone wall next to it. The divine iron hand kept hold of his grasping hand. Everything happened very quickly.

They later found Antonius on the verge of death. His hand lay beside him. It still held the iron God in its stiff fingers.

I have shaken hands with God and he kept mine. As a deposit. The rest will come later, said Antonius and laughed when I met him. This is how I got to know him and his family.

He was in the hospital, which I sometimes went to with a friend. We spoke with the patients there. A lawyer friend from the enemy country, who like Antonius, worked in the peace movement, took care of him. Supported him because the dark clouds had not left him.

Antonius was right in the middle of the thunderstorm. In the hospital he was taken care of. But he did not find peace. He was one of the troublemakers they would like to discharge. He had made himself unpopular. He preached peace and made enemies for himself. He became a danger.

Hate must cease otherwise it will never come to an end, he said.

This made him suspicious in times when peace existed only for a handful of crazies and was felt to be a threat in this power structure.

He was regarded as a traitor by both sides, was a burden to his family and to many of his friends because he was not willing to be an enemy.

When the enemies in his country heard that he had lost his left hand, they laughed scornfully. He had extended his hand to the wrong people, they said, and our God has punished him. We will go and get the rest.

For every group there is a countergroup. Enemies act in groups, fight the enemy and that includes people who think differently. There is an enemy behind every garden wall. The animals eat each other up, some say. You hand over weapons to them. A gun licence in the slaughterhouse. The falcons fly in smaller circles, the pigeons wither in the sky and find no landing place. And a people looking for peace had lost its purpose.

Antonius had got in-between the fronts. His own people were suspicious, because even after his accident he still sought talks with the enemy. Because he believed indefatigably in peace.

One day when he was still in hospital, people came with weapons, killed a doctor and injured a female patient. They said it was intended for him. It was a group from his land. With weapons from the enemy land. They will come back, he was told.

His family asked him to leave, asked me to accompany

him. His farewell was flight. He looked at his land as some-one who will not be coming back.

At Kassim's he found an open door.

The phone is ringing.

Steps go into the ringing. She dries her hands, speaks, nods and nods. Then she comes back. They will be here soon, she says, and dips her hands into the bowl with rice. A milky cloud rises in the water. The rice circulates. She shakes it into a sieve and rinses it before she puts it into a pot with water, adds salt and a few threads of saffron before boiling it.

From a tin she takes out walnuts. Dust comes from a big paper bag of almonds. From a jar pine nuts fall onto the table.

Taste it, Lea. They are from Kassim's land, she says. The reddish brown of the almond skin is the colour of the soil in which they were grown.

They are blanched with boiling water so that the skin comes off. Like a dress that has become too wide, she then says and flicks the light nuts out of their wrinkled skin. An earthy aroma rises from the almonds. The fingers turn brown and her skin shrivels at the tips. The colour gets into the folds and below the nails.

In a pan the nuts are roasting golden brown. The pine nuts are fried separately. They don't take so long. It's done very quickly, she says, and puts the roasted nuts into vari-ous bowls. She leaves some almonds and walnuts in the pan, sprinkles some salt over them and puts them prepared in this way on a small plate.

Taste them, they go well with tea. I'll make some tea for us. It's the right time for it.

She sprinkles big tea leaves in a pot with a handle, pours water on it with a lot of sugar and brings it to the boil.

This tea is being boiled intensively. It is sweetened because it must not be at all bitter.

Then she picks the fresh peppermint leaves from a bunch of herbs and puts them in the glasses.

See what it looks like, Lea. The colour of the tea is greenish red. Because of the peppermint leaves it gets a tart freshness, and afterwards you will forget all your tiredness.

She drinks the hot tea cautiously in small gulps. She keeps filling up Lea's glass. Each time a fresh peppermint leaf is put into the glass.

Mocca and tea. All day long you drink mocca and tea there. There is a time for mocca. There is a time for tea. The time for mocca is followed by the time for tea and the time for tea by the time for mocca. It will be a sacred act every time. Rituals. Mocca or tea are never prepared, boiled, without sending good wishes, without sending devout sayings into the drink. This applies to all meals that are cooked. It cannot be done without good wishes. If they are forgotten the meal will not be successful, it will be burnt, too salty, not easy on the stomach, disappointing for the guest.

The old mother of Mona and her sister, who had come to the new country for a few months to see how things were going for the daughter with the black sheep, sat every day on the bench in front of Kassim's house and drank mocca or tea.

One of them always prepared the mocca, the other the tea. While one of them was in the house to prepare the drink the other sat outside waiting.

While she was waiting, her hands made the prayer chain clatter in her lap. With her head raised, wishes, hopes and gratitude are whispered towards the sky, then her head inclines with eyes closed, to rest on her breast for a while, to listen to her heart.

The other one in the house was whispering, with the same concentration, her sayings into the drink. Then they sat together again with their white, delicate headscarves, lifted their heads at the same time rhythmically like doves swaying on a branch, sipped from the small cups, looked at the land and nodded.

Just as important as the mocca and the tea is the bread.

Flour in a bowl. A little salt drizzled on it. Small hard dots on the white. Her hands prepare the flour, form a hollow.

This was the first thing I ate at Mona's house. Mona prepared fresh bread every day.

She adds the yeast with the lukewarm water to the flour and lets the spongy dough rise. Then she adds some oil and water once again, stirs everything until the dough is smooth and covers the bowl with a cloth. Lea, the bread was also the first thing I ate with Simon at Mona's house. After this he came every day. Kassim brought Simon with him, right after I had come to him with Antonius to take care of his arm. Simon spoke Kassim's and Antonius' language. He came from Kassim's neighbouring village when the land had not yet been divided and everybody could live peacefully together with their religions. After his studies he did not return.

Where should I go? He asked. My land is no longer my land. Strangers have come to my land and turned my friends and neighbours into enemies. They have drawn a line through the land separating us. And turned the line into a wall.

Now his surgery is next door to "The office of all questions. In all languages." It was there that Kassim and Simon got to know each other.

Here is the doctor for Antonius, Kassim said, and Simon shook hands with all of us.

Simon thought at first that Antonius and I were a couple.

She kneads the dough until bubbles rise.

Mona came with the bread, the tea and invited him to stay for the meal. We both reached for the same piece of bread. We looked at each other, we laughed and shared it. Then we knew.

The dough sticks to the rim of the bowl. She covers her hands with flour and kneads it until it is smooth and separates from the bottom of the bowl. Pours oil over her white fingers, spreads it inside the bowl, shapes the dough to form a shiny ball.

It will double in size she says, she puts the ball into the bowl and covers it with a cloth.

Kassim had to buy chairs.

When Mona's sister lost her husband as well, she came to him with her two children. They should have a future, Kassim said and opened his house.

They had escaped the turmoil and found a place at Kassim's table. For Mona and Kassim it was a happy event whenever the family grew bigger. Nothing gave them more security in the new land, nothing strengthened their roots as much as a big family. Family and land – they belonged together. The more members of the family Kassim took care of, the more his land grew. Kassim provided work for all of them, he needed them and was able to take care of them all.

Mona was glad when her sister came. It was a good feeling to have a woman around who spoke the same language and to whom one was bound by a common history. Working together. Setting the table, talking, feeling at home with one other. A small cup of mocca, ready to have its coffee grounds read. What has been. What is. What will be.

When they sat together in the evening at the big table on one of the first days, Mona and her sister had noticed it at the same time.

As on every evening, they all sat together. Mona and Kassim, their children, Mona's brother Antonius, and her sister with the two almost grown-up children, a few cousins from a different branch of the family who helped Kassim with the harvest, Mona's old mother with her sister, the aunt.

They all saw him coming. Walking up the road along the path of roses to the house. He came to welcome the new members of the family. He had become a friend who belonged to the family. Joseph had become indispensible for Kassim. Just as Kassim in turn had become indispensible for him. "JoKa" it said on the "Office for all questions. In all languages". "JoKa" was written on the doors of the offices, the warehouses, the lorries. They both had made "JoKa" into a trading company which was known well beyond the borders. Kassim and Joseph always laughed when they met and put their palms together by way of a greeting, held each other by the shoulders and looked at each other before they started to talk.

When Joseph came, it was not yet evening. The sun was just disappearing behind the mountains. The sky was changing colour to yellow. A shadowless bright light.

Kassim got up and went towards Joseph, then they held each other by the shoulders and laughed. Kassim turned round, They are here, he said and pointed to Mona's sister and her two children.

Joseph welcomed the sister. He welcomed her son. But he had eyes only for the daughter. Nadja. It was difficult for him not to keep looking in her direction. And she had learnt to lower her eyes.

Twilight came quickly. Their eyes looked steadily and lingered longer on the person opposite. When the lights were switched on it became visible. The two sisters looked at each other. They had noticed it. Even in the soft light of the candles you saw the red on Nadja's cheeks when Joseph said good-bye to her and left.

After that Joseph came every day. Sometimes only for a few minutes. Sometimes he brought something from the supermarket for Mona. Sometimes he came with his father. Then they sat with Kassim at the big table and looked over the land, and Joseph always kept looking up at a window. He was familiar with the place. He knew the house. The two sisters noticed his glances. They noticed his interest. Nadja also noticed it.

Nadja's table was at the window. She bent over the books and read. She had taken them out again after leaving her country with her mother and younger brother. Over the years the university in her country had had to close its gates for months at a time because of the disturbances. Even the schools and other institutes often remained closed.

Life was difficult there for the adults. And for the young ones and the children it was difficult to find meaning and motivation for the future. It was hard for the parents to keep their children at home. The protests on the streets against the despotism of foreign rule created new victims every day.

When Nadja sat at the window, she did not only look at

her books. She also gazed over the landscape which appeared familiar from the first day onwards, and this was mixed with positive images in her memory which she had brought with her, and which lived on.

She looked at the land, saw the colours, felt the warm wind, smelt the scent of the soil day and night. Then she took a deep breath and had the feeling that she had never breathed before, had held her breath, and concealed it and only now, in this new land, in this new room, seated by the window, she began to breathe as if liberated. A gift, she thought, and sank back in the chair in relief.

It seemed to her as if she had broken through an insurmountable wall which had prevented her from living. Here the landscape was a landscape.

The street was a street. And it didn't represent the danger of being chased by persecutors, who threatened them from their armoured vehicles with their special missiles.

It was not the street which suddenly came to an end because of barriers, or which one was not allowed to walk on at certain times.

It was not the street which scared her out of her wits, which she could not cross safely either on her own or with others.

It wasn't the street on which one's own vehicles were marked with special signs in order to be clearly identified by the persecutors.

Streets which became a dangerous disease which everyone wanted to avoid if at all possible. Streets where groups of children ran wild, who played a war game because of their hopelessness. Streets which she had known all her life only as a place of extreme danger.

A hill was not a hill. It could be the place from which alien eyes looked and monitored the next morning. When moaning vehicles startled the night, the inhabitants knew what was happening. They knew the vehicles, they knew their load, the rectangular blocks. A dozen or more and overnight a village never seen before emerged. The constructors put up their ready-made houses, their ready-made kindergartens, ready-made schools, ready-made fountains, ready-made electricity, ready-made walls and watchtowers and they rolled out their ready-made spools of their special barbed wire.

And ready-made families were standing in this ready-made village in the morning and hanging up their washing.

A bush was not a bush. It was something dangerous in the garden, in front of the house, on the street, where the next terror could lurk. Around the houses, in the gardens, everything was bare.

A house was no longer a home. It didn't mean protection anymore, and certainly not safety. Even the parents did not mean protection. They could not guarantee it. The children noticed from the beginning the helplessness like a constant shadow. They were all equally vulnerable. The nights of the recent years did not mean peace but anguish. The morning after everything could be different.

Nights spent awake after the doors and windows had been barred in the evening and wedged with slats, when alien boots paced around the house and the family listened in the sleepless hours to unknown voices.

Nadja was familiar with the fear. This breathlessness. The whole country held its breath. Often she wanted to be away from it all. In her life things had shifted. Nothing was as it should be.

The view from the window now showed her a world as it could be. She saw the colours of the fields in the morning in the haze shining, green, with dew, heard the cocks crowing by the house and crowing back in the distance, the twittering of the birds in the bushes and trees, she had forgotten this. She heard the laughter of the children in the landscape, saw Mona's children frolicking around with her brother in the garden and cycling down the street to the next village where they played, without a care, forgotten games, with a naturalness unknown to her and with this right to freedom which had only been a word for her. A distant word, a term, no more, too unreal for her to grasp.

Complete calm lay over the fields when she looked out of the window at midday and the air beneath the hot sky was dancing. At night she now opened it wide, let the air come in and began to breathe without fear. The murmuring of the pines softened the chirping of the crickets, sometimes near, sometimes far away. The murmuring of the pines was the murmuring of the night. The windows stayed open. The night became a new concept for her and lost its menace. Nadja was amazed at the sound of silence, which was wrapped around her consciousness like a bandage and calmed her down. Only when she felt an unknown freshness after waking up and when painful dreams did not overwhelm her, did she trust the night and longed for sleep.

Slowly her anger left her thoughts, and she felt futility when she thought about those who turned her and her people into enemies and were poisoned through this, and she felt her anger vanish like an illness.

She felt she had escaped. She felt she had escaped from her persecutors, who were themselves persecuted and who no longer felt appalled by what they were suffering, who had lost, had sold their history and had let it be used. Relief set their thoughts free and spread like recovery.

With each day Nadja's gazes could range more widely. She let herself be guided by what she saw. There were days which she awaited in hopeful excitement, which she greeted in the morning with impatience, as if she was receiving a letter and beginning to read it. The gazes struck her. They struck her everywhere, not only when she saw them. The gazes set her alight, the red colour flashed to the tips of her hair, they were there even when she kept her eyes closed. Everything could be read.

It is high time, her sisters will have said, while they were shaping the rolls of wine leaves in the kitchen.

She goes back and forth. Clattering of pot lids on the cooker. Stirring. Tasting. She closes her eyes when doing this and nods. Bowls are washed up. The working surface is cleaned. In front of the mirror she puts her fingers through her hair.

She has gone into the garden and cut herbs once again.

A bunch of green stuff, she says. Curly parsley leaves with their strong stalks are the basis of every dish with herbs. Although they look so headstrong, they go together well with the other herbs, enhance the strange taste and add volume. Dill, delicately feathered, sways in the bunch as if it were coy. It reacts sensitively and becomes weak quickly if it is not carefully handled. Chives crunch with their stiff greenery. Their yellowish tips stick out of the bunch. They stand their ground among the variety of shapes and spray out their sharp colour when they are cut. The furry green of mint is mild, is conciliatory and unfolds when fresh or cooked, a breath of summer freshness.

She washes the herbs, removes the yellow tips of the leaves and stalks and puts them in the strainer to drip dry. Later she will cut everything into small pieces, and mix shallots, tomatoes, cucumber, with lemon juice, olive oil with salt, pepper and a little honey and the soft couscous to make a refreshing salad.

Out of a basket she takes the big onions, strips off the rustling skin and cuts the onions into cubes. In the pan they are fried golden-brown.

Kibbeh must not be missing. With the kibbeh the surprise

comes in the middle, you take a bite and the filling seduces you to eat more than you should.

Lean mince is kneaded together with soaked bulgur, a finely cut onion, salt, crushed pimento seeds, cumin, a pinch of cinnamon and black pepper are added. After she has moistened her hands with water, she takes some of the mince, shapes it into small balls, presses a hole into it with her thumb, fills it with roasted pine nuts and onions from the pan. Then she closes the hole and turns the small ball into a longish shape. They are fried and then rest dark brown in a dish.

Taste a kibbeh.

She has laid out some small ones.

They taste good, both warm and cold. Some of them we'll dip in yoghurt sauce.

She takes a small kibbeh ball, holds it between her thumb and index finger and bites the top off. A few nuts fall onto her.

That's the way I like it. Quite mild, then you can taste the pine nuts.

She cuts onions and a garlic clove very finely. They are stirred in a pot with butter until the onions are translucent. Some flour is dissolved in the broth. It becomes a smooth sauce, a little pepper and salt, and then she pours yoghurt in while stirring. It must not come to the boil anymore. She takes the sauce from the cooker and pours it into a bowl. A little lemon juice and melissa, and she puts some kibbeh into it.

As you can see, Lea, these meals take time. Time which the sisters needed to understand them. To make them their confidants. In order to rediscover the familiar during this time together, to find each other. The ingredients for the daily meals, the smells, the colours, the whole variety connects you to the land on which all of that has grown.

The sisters go outside. They find the herbs in the garden. They smell the mint, the rosemary, the thyme. Aroma from the past. Orient, they say, with their eyes closed, and think about their homeland, as it sounds like a word from a rediscovered time. They remember.

They harvest the vegetables which they grew themselves, rub the leaves of the tomato plants between their fingers, skin the stalks of thick thistles, a bitter-sweet taste. They remember.

Lingering in the shadow of the pines, listening to the never-ending murmuring, the gentle whistling which the pines make even without any movement of the air. Ragged carnations in the flower bed. Nutmeg. The colour of the landscape. They long for the landscape. Red soil sticks to their shoes. They remember.

Everything is there, but at the same time evokes longing for it. When does it start to be homeland? When does what is strange become familiar?

The sisters' eyes look at Joseph and are full of questions.

The women were unprepared, therefore uncertain and perplexed at first. All their attention was suddenly focussed on the glances which Joseph had for Nadja. Glances which were signs. They were tolerated because one did not know how to deal with them. They were observed and acknowledged.

On the one hand they knew of course that there would be glances one day, on the other they were irritated because they were used to directing glances before they started. On the one hand Joseph was the friend who belonged to the family, on the other he was the man who was a stranger.

Not a word was said about it yet. The sisters were still waiting for the glances of Kassim who ignored all the glances which went back and forth, received the glances of the women, but did not react to them.

The women waited. By saying nothing they also said nothing in favour of it and nothing against it.

Nadja escaped their watchfulness by allowing all the glances. She accepted Joseph's glances, she accepted those of her mother, her aunt, her grandmother, her great-aunt, Kassim and Antonius. The children laughed and did not hide their laughter. Nadja smiled back. She soon put an end to all mistrust, and the women found pleasure in strange ideas and connected their thoughts to ever-changing images reaching into the future, which no longer seemed unforeseeably strange. The sisters had learnt to think practically, and also to allow for chance. They not only caught the glances, they looked beyond them and looked through them into a new time.

The new time was approaching.

Thoughts took new directions. Days became long and full, fell out of the mist of the morning and ended in the blue of the night.

Nadja's glances were intensely alert. The brief time in the new land had been enough to show her what a life in freedom and security can be like. When she saw Mona's children playing, she understood what she had painfully missed, what up to then had remained completely unknown to her. She knew what she wanted: her right to a free life, and, should she have children, they should be allowed to grow up without fear, also for the sake of the parents.

She said yes when Joseph asked her and went down to the "Office for all questions. In all languages" and to the library of the town nearby, which had been her wish.

Glances from the house beyond the playing children, beyond the terrace, down the path to the road. On the road the car rolled on with the couple, a dark dot, over the mountain and disappeared behind the next bend.

On the way down there was the spring.

Joseph had forgotten nothing. It was important for him to show Nadja this spot. He took her to the spring of his ancestors which had its source there, not far from where they were. He went in order to show the narrow path a short distance in front of her, across the field which now belonged to Kassim. Thick bushes beneath the eucalyptus trees which rustled in the warm wind and rubbed their silvery twigs against each other and cast shadowy spots over the field. Rosemary, wild broom, silver poppy and oleander grew around the trees like a hedge. Birds flew up from the bushes and noisily looked for perches in the leaves on high branches and twigs.

Joseph spread out his arms to open up the path, which was overgrown and ended in front of twigs. He found the way in, bent the bushes to one side, showed Nadja a paved path.

They had stepped into a different light. It fell through the green trees which concealed the blue of the sky.

The old stone slabs beneath their feet were damp and slippery here. Fern and moss poured out of the gaps and revealed their footsteps as a dark trace. A grey shadow was cast by the edge of the wall, which was old, fissured and raw. A forgotten wall. Apparently a dead end. Joseph knew the wall. Plants had fought against it, had lodged and found their place in the grooves and folds.

Joseph knew the end of the wall and Nadja saw at first only a bright line as if someone had drawn a line with a steady hand. It came from the gap at the entrance of the inner courtyard of the spring.

There were no plants there anymore. Light and shade had clear shapes. Steps led deep down to a round space carved into the rock, which opened like a tower to the sky.

From a hole in the rock flowed clear water in a groove, babbled into a pool, and on the other side of the pool back into the rock. On the outside it then left the rock after a few metres and continued its way visibly as a brook in paved channels.

Nadja felt the coolness of the spring. Warm light rested only on the stone bench. Many had already sat there. Joseph knew the story and related how his family had settled here many hundreds of years ago because of the spring, how everything started and how everything was about the water, even at that time.

Nadja will have listened and perhaps she will have begun to tell her story.

The sun drew shadows on the stone bench. Red fiery flowers sparkled over Nadja's dress. Gazes met. The distance was suddenly very near. Then Nadja bent forward and drank water from the spring. She could not stop drinking it. It was not only thirst which made her drink this water, as if she had never drunk water before.

They continued on foot across the land, along the small brook, through an olive grove, across the fields down to the road.

Like a piece of sky, the water lay there in a basin. Smooth and shimmering. Bright clouds darted over it and passed across the edge of the basin as dark shadows. The spring water nourished the land around it. Old channels led it further across the fields until it flowed in a paved bed slowly down to the sea and disappeared in it.

When they reached the house again late in the afternoon the two women looked at Nadja. It is high time, Mona said to her sister and set the plates and bowls for the meal in the evening.

Joseph drove down the mountain. He waved out of the window. A cloud of dust rose behind his car and settled down again only after he had long disappeared.

She takes the dough out of the dish. It has grown into a big ball.

She kneeds the dough once again and removes small pieces from it, presses them flat and puts them on a cloth dusted with flour.

They have to rise for another twenty minutes. Only then are they put into the hot oven and baked on both sides. The pieces of bread are briefly browned, but should be light on the inside and have a pocket in the middle which you can cut open and fill. Simply with salad, falafel, kibbeh and tahini sauce – whatever you want. I shall spread a paste on some pieces of bread beforehand which are eaten like pizza and best when they are still warm in your hand.

She takes the stones out of the black olives, cuts up the pulp. She spreads a smooth paste which is made with pine nuts, thyme, pepper, salt, and a little oil on the flat pieces of bread. She presses skinned tomatoes, cut into small cubes, and feta into the filling and pushes the pieces of bread into the oven.

One evening Kassim was standing outside and looked at his watch, then at the road, which crept up the mountain-side like a thin grey snake that warmed itself in the late light. He turned round and went into the house to get two chairs and put them to the right and left of his chair at the table.

Mona and her sister walked back and forth. Nadja was in the house. The heat of the day had not yet gone. It spread out its warm blanket over the evening. The two old ones, the mother, the aunt, were sitting on the bench in front of the house. They loved the warmth. Not the heat of the midday, but the warmth of the late afternoon and evening in the shadow of the wall of the house. They loved this warmth. They were familiar with it. They felt it doing them good, and missed it when it was cool.

They whispered to each other. They held their hands before their mouths. They laughed secretly. They sat side by side, their arms touching. Their feet did not reach the floor. They ended just before it and swung from time to time back and forth. Both women had enormous breasts. A mountain range which started to bulge under their chins and now, when they were leaning forward, rested like a cushion on their thighs. Underneath the dark material one could see their thighs like bulging cushions. Their movements were agile and quick. Their speech was agile and quick. Their eyes. Their fingers. They kept moving the pearls of their prayer chains incessantly.

Antonius came round with a carafe of lemon water. Walking past he picked mint leaves, rubbed them a little and put them in.

How are you, he said to the two old ones and put the carafe on the table. They thanked him and asked in turn how things were, and Antonius nodded.

How are things, Kassim also asked whenever he went past

them. They thanked him in unison and asked back, how are things.

Mona and her sister, coming out of the kitchen, walked back and forth, past the old ones, how are you, how are you, back and forth.

The children poked little sticks carefully into the gaps in the wall, tried to catch green shimmering lizards. They ran to the old ones, how are things, thank you, thank you, and showed them their lizard house made of cardboard. They listened together and heard the lizards rustling between the moss and the twigs.

The warmth lingered in the house as well. The door, a breathing mouth. The sisters were breathed in and out and carried the warmth with them and on their trays in and out all day long.

Kassim looked at his watch again. The road was in a yellow light now, and right at the bottom he recognized a black dot which slowly became bigger. The two old ones saw it as well, nodded and let the chains slip eagerly through their fingers. The children put the lizard's house down into the moss and frolicked around the table. Mona also recognized the dot. Soon she could hear that it was Joseph's car. She looked at the table.

The meal would be plentiful. They had had a lot to speak about, all day long, they had cooked a lot. The sister joined them and they both smoothed out their dresses and their hair with similar movements. They were excited. They both knew why.

The children waved and rushed towards the car.

When Joseph and his father got out, Kassim greeted both of them with an embrace and led them to the table. Each on one side of his chair. Finally they were all seated. Mona and her sister served the food, Kassim poured the drinks, the two old ones shifted their chairs in between the children. Nadja put the bread on the table.

The table stood in the blue of the evening. The food was the field, the land, the water, the sea. The wine in the glass spread its red colour. Lingering gazes which found words, thoughts grew and became wide and clear.

When the men had shaken hands, Nadja made the coffee. She poured it in small cups without handles, and while she looked into the dark colour as into a mirror she passed the cup with the thickest foam to Joseph. Then the women went with the children into the house.

The night had many voices left and the lights did not go out till it was late. Outside, as well as behind the windows.

That night their sleep will have been furrowed by dreams and the following morning, which looked like all the other mornings before, they will all have experienced a completely new morning.

The light was between night and day, when Kassim got up. Every morning he used the time in-between and loved the sounds which only then could be heard because they were otherwise swallowed up by other sounds, or it was not time for them anymore. He loved the smells which rose from the damp soil and he could smell the fertility of the fields, the trees, the whole garden. Like his grandfather he was able to tell from the smell when the harvest was ready on the fields, when the fruit on the tree was ripe. He smelt the colour of a rose. The early morning was fresh and cool, and always cleared his head for new thoughts. And with his hand he wiped the dew from his chair outside by the table before he sat down. There were no shadows yet. Only the idea of their colour lay over everything. He saw the mist on the horizon clearing and waited for the light of day.

A few hours further east the sun already stood over his land. Lit up his abandoned fields, his trees, his hills and meadows, the houses of his ancestors. Everything was suffused by light.

And he saw the farmers on the plain driving over the fields with their tractors, saw the workers standing together in groups, the shepherd leading his herd from the plain up the hill to the olive grove. There was light on the roofs of the houses in the valley, close to the monastery and the mosque. He heard the noise of the children in the school yard, saw the women running back and forth between the ovens and the first smoke rising. A bus crept chugging up the hill.

He kept his eyes closed and could see everything. Everything was clearly visible. Time had made him patient.

One day, he said, one day we will see all this again. One

day we will return to our country. We shall manage to be united. One day my son will also return. Then he will know how to sow and harvest, and will not come with empty hands.

One day. He believed in this.

He opened his eyes and saw the bluish-white mist over the new land turning into the bluish-white of the sky. He saw the rising arch which divided land and sky, the narrow edge of a circle which quickly grew to become a red disc and immediately coloured everything. He felt the warmth as soon as the red became visible. The sky was now the background of the disc. It had changed its colour. The white sky became blue. The mist lay damp on the plants. In the valley the dew was steaming and drifted in delicate streaks over the fields.

It was an interim time of the day when the morning was still fresh. It was the time to start the daily chores, the time when the day had begun, its course still open and to be determined by the actions of each individual.

The red of her cape was the colour of the sun when Mona came through the door with the mocca. As on every morning, Kassim and Mona drank the first coffee together in front of the house. They both sat side by side and looked at the bright landscape. It looked just as on the days before, but it seemed to them completely new today.

They sat at their table in front of their house on their land, on which everything grew as on the land which they called their homeland. What was distant was suddenly very near and grew together with the land they were looking at.

Kassim got up and walked along the path which he took every morning.

Mona gazed after him. She watched him leaving. She saw his shoulders. She knew. This morning he distanced himself a bit further from the time of the old land and crossed over into the time of the new land.

The landscape was not just a picture.

Someone shouted from the window. Sister waved to sister. She should stay. At the table in front of the house. When she came she brought out fresh coffee. Then they sat side by side, as Mona had sat before with Kassim. They felt the soil underneath their feet. They had rested their arms on the wooden table, held their cups up to their mouths and drank in small sips. They did not talk either. They looked at the land.

Fields were fields. Trees were trees. Hills were hills. A group of houses was crowded around a spring. It had been like this there too.

The image was a landscape.

They looked into it.

The transparent light had disappeared. The morning was getting up and overturned their distant images.

A different time, Mona said and looked into the changed light. For them it was as if they had not exchanged the land but calmed, smoothed and reawakened everything to life with a generous hand. That's how it could have been. Just as it was now.

The women had experienced much more quickly what

it means to spend the day in peace. When they could abandon their fear, grief also went away, and they were ready to let themselves be comforted.

They had found again what they had lost. They had found life again. Although they did not want to express it openly, it was clear to them after only a few weeks in the new land. That morning, when they drank their coffee together at the table outside, the new land was an open house for them.

They did not say anything. They just looked inside. They both knew it about each other. Maybe they had no words for it. They both had a daring expression, as if they had been thinking about something forbidden. Later they laughed, saw the children coming. They went into the house to prepare the meal.

I remember the sweet dishes, Lea, she says, and takes a big bowl from the cupboard. The sweet dish at the end is just as important as everything that went before.

Six eggs. She breaks open half of them and puts them into the bowl, from the others she only takes the yolk. With sugar and milk she stirs it to a foamy mixture.

Crème caramel, Lea, it's part of it. She scrapes the pulp out of the vanilla pods. What a delicate aroma is hidden in the black pods.

She bends over and breathes it in. It spreads in the room. The aroma is lily. Full blossom. A fresh bunch.

She scrapes the black crumbs out of the pods into the light cream.

On the wedding table this was one of many bowls. Dishes were constantly being served, eaten, cleared away, served anew.

The sweetness must be intoxicating.

The sweet dishes lay on a bed of flowers. Blossoms were spread all over the table and were artistically arranged in patterns. Green paths led to diamonds, clubs, hearts, broke through circles, and the cakes, as if on stilts, were floating on top in the colours of the blossoms. Thin strips of pastry, thread-like, rolled around different nuts. Crèmes, foamy mixtures, which released an aroma of roses, each tree had donated its fruits, whole bushes were relieved of their berries and lay sweetened with sugar, glazed in jars.

Kassim had got hold of a tent.

It was as big as a house and made of the same material as kilims. A wedding tent. That's how they celebrated in his country. It was supposed to be the first big festivity in the new land – in a tent from his old land. Days before the celebration Kassim and Joseph had set it up with several other men. The children played circus inside, chased the dogs, cats, sheep through the tent through one opening and out through the other. The olds ones sat in it, when the sun was at its highest, and smelt the homeland. They sat under the roof of the homeland in a foreign land, drank tea or mocca and held their prayer chains ready on their laps.

Nadja saw the tent from her window. She saw the dark opening of the folded-back flap. She knew that the other one was in the light and led to the road outside and that she would no longer be a stranger when she had gone through this opening.

She thought about the rituals. The hamam, the henna painting, the women's celebration. About the night before.

The hamam will be a bathroom. The henna painter will be the aunt. The women's celebration will be the day before and the night before will become the night afterwards. Rituals change.

They will soon come, Lea.

The light is slanted in the room. The sun is over the corn. The tree in the field is a grey spot. The sky looks back.

She caramelizes cubes of sugar in a pot, adds finely cut strips of orange peel and some orange juice.

That's how I saw it done by Mona, she says, pours the sauce into a heat-resistant form and spreads the egg mixture over it. Everything is heated up in a water-bath and is then put into the oven until it becomes solid. When it cools down the sweet dish is overturned onto a plate.

She sees from the kitchen, the dining area, illuminated by the slanting light.

This is how the evening begins. It moves from the land-scape into the house and spreads out. She arranges plates and glasses and when she comes back, having changed her clothes, the table is already set.

Borders are no longer walls. In only a few hours everybody was sitting together at one table.

How did you prepare it, asks Mona and looks at the dishes. They are familiar to her.

I have learnt everything from you, she says to her and to Mona's sister at the same time.

She passes the bread to Simon, he looks at it and nods.

It is evening. The new light changes the look of the room. The starters emit their aroma. Eyes are busy taking in the various colours. Kassim puts the wine on the table. Joseph and Nadja light the fire in the grill.

Antonius sits opposite Lea. They talk to each other. Lea about her parents' land. Lea says that her parents' land is not her land, that her land is not her parents' land.

Antonius nods. He talks about his land which is the land of her and his parents, and about the hope of a life together. He talks about the land, in which he now has found room to live, which is the land of his friends. Lea nods.

Outside the night is a dark cloth. Inside the table sails through the room. Lea makes mocca. Sugar, cardamom, coffee, water. She stirs. The coffee surges up.

She speaks into it in a low voice. Her words will be wishes. She pours the mocca into the little cups without handles. She passes the little cups round. She passes the last one with the thickest foam to Antonius. Antonius looks at her.

"Holy was the land for all"

Stories of flight, expulsion and disenfranchisement, loss of family and home, death and sadness, hope and hopelessness. Stories of people who all have their names, their idiosyncrasies and contradictions, desires and dreams – not carriers of ethnic labels, of victim roles or heroism. Not even the word "Palestine" or "Israel" is mentioned.

Yet the narrative hides nothing; on the contrary, it gives the misery and suffering in "this beguiling, bleeding landscape" an expressive, multi-faceted face.

"The home of these people is their memory. They keep telling them so that nothing is forgotten." Especially at such a wedding dinner: "They had a lot to talk about all day, had cooked a lot", before the table was set in the blue of the evening. And "never will a mocha or tea be served without sending good wishes, pious sayings into the drink. It will not work without the good wishes."

Karin Irshaid tells about it with poetic, sensual pictures and in a warm tone. And it is unmistakably partisan – for the country that once was "holy to all".

Niko Ewers

KIENER
PRESS
London, UK, info@kiener-press.com

Karin Irshaid:
The Wedding Feast
ISBN 978-3-943324-85-3

Translation into English by Paul Crichton and Christl Kiener of "Das Hochzeitsessen",
3rd edition 2015 (ISBN 978-3-943324-91-4) KIENER-Verlag, München

© 2019 by KIENER Press

A CIP record for this book is available from the British Library.

Typesetting: Kadja Gericke, Arnstorf/Germany
Printed and bound by: Drukarnia Dimograf Sp. z o.o., Bielsko-Biała/Poland
Cover design: SpieszDesign, Neu-Ulm/Germany
Cover illustration: Karin Irshaid

www.kiener-press.com